Garden Party Ghostess

THORN HOUSE ROAD MYSTERIES
BOOK 1

EMILY FLUKE

Copyright © 2023 by Emily Fluke

All rights reserved.

No part of this book may be reproduced in any form or by any electronic or mechanical means, including information storage and retrieval systems, without written permission from the author, except for the use of brief quotations in a book review.

ALSO BY EMILY FLUKE

-Thorn House Road Mysteries

Garden Party Ghostess

Wedding Party Witness (releasing 2024)

-The Mari Fable Mysteries

Death of a Fairy Tale

Kidnapping the Classics

The Pinocchio Project

A Grimm Haunting

Snow Spell's Heartbreak

Book 6 (releasing 2024)

-The Bewitcher's Beach Paranormal Cozy Mystery Series

Magic, Movies, and Murder (releasing October 2023)

Summoning, Skating, and Skulls (releasing soon)

Book 3 (releasing soon)

-Folklore Falls Romance Retellings

Until Theft Do Us Part

Fake Dating's a Beast

Be sure to snag the prequels to both the Mari Fable Mysteries, and the Bewitcher's Beach Paranormal Cozy Mysteries FREE from my newsletter: The Glass Coffin and Be Careful What You Witch For.

https://landing.mailerlite.com/webforms/landing/y4h6c8

"To all the readers who fancy themselves sleuths.

Can we be friends?"

1
AT THE HOUSE WITH A HOST

Ghosts aren't real, but homes hold memories of those who lived before, and this house's hideous crown molding hinted at its ugly past. I trail my finger along the dusty banister. The black walnut wood reveals every speck of dirt and grime, and I decide it'll be the first change I make to prove to the neighborhood that this house isn't haunted.

"Say your last goodbyes," I tell the banister as I knock my fist against it a little too hard. My knuckle throbs and I give the walnut wood my best evil eye. "Feisty one, huh? Well, you've never dealt with the famous Olive Glass."

I attempt a maniacal laugh, the side of myself rarely shown on screen when I starred in Renovation Station. Spit lodges in my throat and I have to stop to cough, glaring at the banister as if it's judging me.

I might be a little sensitive after the home improvement network dropped me for "having a bubbly personality that overshadows the focus of the show," which really meant I didn't bring enough drama to my episodes. That and the fact that they took the show in another direction, calling it

Rose and Hose Renovation. Apparently, garden makeovers are all the rage, and I don't have the eye for plants—or rather, the thumb for greens.

Inheriting this house, though hideous, came in the nick of time when a lost job meant eviction. It's the lesser of two evils, even though it involved accepting my dead ex-boyfriend's family home in the town I abandoned after getting pregnant during prom.

"Exes over eviction," I mumble.

I sigh and rest my hands on my hips, the way a mother stands when she scolds her child. Thankfully, my daughter is an angel, and in her fifteen years of life, I've rarely had to scold her.

Instead, it's houses, like this one, that I've had to whip into shape. Though out of the dozens of homes I've given makeovers, none have come with claims of ghost sightings.

A figure appears at the top of the staircase that mirrors where I stand. My heart leaps into my throat as I stare across the space into what feels like a reflection.

A face nearly identical to mine—but eighteen years younger—smiles back at me.

"Demolition!" I curse creatively. "Zyra, you almost made me pee my pants. Stomp so I can hear you coming next time."

My daughter rolls her eyes and huffs. "I'm almost an adult, Mom, you can say real cuss words around me."

"Demolition *is* a bad word," I insist. "Because if a house is so far gone that it needs to be—"

"Demolished, then it means I've failed my life's calling." Zyra finishes the quote for me. "Yeah, yeah, whatever." Though her teen attitude peeks out, I see the grin her crossed arms and peaked eyebrow can't hide. "So." Though she snaps the textbook in her hand shut, she keeps her finger in place as a bookmark. She hops down the steps that look to belong in a palace, not a home on Thorn House Road. "Are we going to survive the night?"

I walk down the steps, meeting her at the halfway landing between the imperial-style staircase where two symmetrical stairs face one another.

"It's not haunted," I say, though I avoid the gaze of the people in the giant painting above the landing. I like to think I'm brave, but I don't even want to look at the spooky portrait. "Now the fact that my favorite sweater looks better on you? That's haunting me."

Zyra wiggles her shoulders in a little dance. The words on the sweatshirt have faded, but I can still make out the cheesy saying: *20% iced coffee, 80% interior designer*.

When she turns to the painting, I'm reminded of what's really haunting me. Zyra isn't daunted by the family portrait of a modern, but regal-looking man with his wife and son beside him. To her, the boy is a distant image of a man considered her father. To me, the sight of even his boyish face comes with a million emotions. Tomorrow, after I tear down the heavy velvet curtains ruining the entry and let sunlight in, I'll have the guts to take down that painting.

"That's not what everyone in the neighborhood claimed," she says. She shakes overgrown bangs from her face that have faded from the dyed purple to a silver that shines against her naturally dark hair.

I fold my arms. "Remind me not to bring you to the next HOA meeting."

"What does HOA stand for, anyway?"

"Homeowners' Association," I say, as I turn to the rest of the steps and leave her to stare at the painting.

"If they legitimately want to tear the house down

because of evil spirits, don't you think we should listen?" Her voice bounces off the wall and carries into the open space of the massive entry, where a chandelier has turned from glittering glory to a haunted cliche with dozens of cobwebs strung across its crystals.

"That's just an excuse for them to get rid of the community eyesore so their property values go up," I say, as I pull a wrinkled blanket from a cardboard box. The dozen or so boxes in front of me are the culmination of my life's contents. Years of dedicating myself to professional interior design made me a minimalist for aesthetic purposes. Now, it just looks sad.

I trace my finger along the edge of an old photo album at the bottom of the box labeled *bedroom*. Years ago, I collected the images and intended to send the album to her father. I even added our high school prom photos. It's included alongside the picture of him holding Zyra for the first time, only months after our graduation. And months before I left this town behind.

Zyra hops up behind me and plants a kiss on my cheek, which is easy since she's an inch taller than me now.

"I'm going to bed before the spooks come out," she says, pointing to the bare mattress through the sitting room doorway. At my instruction, the movers dropped it in front of the old fireplace rather than dragging it upstairs to the cold bedrooms.

Despite the preparations I made, like changing our address and activating the power, the house fell into disrepair and we quickly discovered the heater didn't work.

I spin and throw my arms around her. The boy's eyes in the portrait seem to shift to meet mine. His shade of sienna matches both the fireplace's mantel and Zyra's eyes. I know that shade of brown based on the swatch of paint I once compared his eyes to all those years ago. We planned the house we'd buy together someday, but that was before he dropped me—and our daughter—like a hot potato.

"You're choking me," Zyra says, coughing and wheezing dramatically as she pulls away. "Forget the haunted house, I'm more worried about you."

I roll my eyes. Maybe that's where she learned the attitude. *Oops.*

I follow her into the massive sitting room to the right of the entry where the ceiling is peaked, and heavy dark bookshelves line the walls.

"I mean that in more ways than one," she says as she dumps her pillow and a blanket on the mattress. We pushed it as close to the fireplace as possible to stay warm tonight. "I saw you eyeing the flannel guy at the HO-whatever meeting. Don't break another poor guy's heart, Mom."

"I was not eyeing him." I shake my head and crouch in front of the fireplace. I bought an easy-light log from the little grocer just outside the suburb but failed to locate a lighter. "He just reminds me of an actor or something. I was trying to place him."

"Right." She laughs and pulls the blanket to her armpits, leaving her hands free to tap away on her cell phone. "That's a bigger lie than me saying I love the fact we don't get service inside this monstrosity."

"Good," I say, though it's very *not* good. It's quite terrible, in fact, considering I planned to ease my anxiety with a late-night addiction to Penthouse Prop-up, the stupid home improvement game that has me spending way too many hours on my phone. If ghosts are watching us, they'll probably think I'm the teenager and Zyra's the responsible one. "This gives you an excuse to take a study break."

"I'm going to take a consciousness break," she says with a yawn. "Goodnight."

I crawl into the bed beside her, dragging the blanket that I hope will be warm enough since the fireplace is still dark.

Despite the chilly room and the poorly installed modern ceiling fan staring down at me, I'm comfortable. Soon, Zyra's rhythmic breathing has me jealous. I need all the sleep I can get after the cross-country move to the little neighborhood known as Thorn House Road—a place I didn't visit often since I saw those two blue lines on a pregnancy test.

After tossing and turning, I roll off the mattress and dig a jacket out of a box in the entry. I pull it on and slip out the front door. Hopefully, fresh air and planning renovations for the exterior will distract me as well as Penthouse Propup usually does. While I don't design the outside of homes professionally, I've decided a good challenge will lift my spirits.

"Spirits," I whisper, my breath turning white against the night's cool spring air, "are not real." Though saying it doesn't make it so. The truth is, I've felt a lingering chill since we stepped foot inside Thorn House.

I refuse to think too deeply about it. I don't need my baby daddy or his late judgmental family haunting my every step. Somehow, the paperwork slipped away, and the fact that my high school sweetheart left this house to me and Zyra was forgotten, until now.

I rub my hands together and walk around the outside of the three-story home. The garden in the back is just as impressive with its acres of hedges, though it's overgrown and in disrepair itself.

A tacky, modern-looking deck is attached to the old

mansion in the back, overlooking an open space of weedy grass. The eyesore deck is made worse by mismatched wood panels in one square section near the house's back door. For now, I plan to cover it with a doormat, though I don't think I'll find one large enough. Tall, thick hedges line the edge of the lawn to the entrance of the massive, infamous maze built—but never explained—by my ex's father.

I hug my arms around my torso and wade through the weeds. The hedges form a massive, dark maze I chose to forget about long ago. Not to mention the spooky vibes of the towering gate and black iron fence that surround the acres of maze, to which I've yet to locate a key. Thankfully, the gate sits open, almost as if held there by the hands of the vines that have grown and curled around its pointed spires.

Despite the spookiness, I'm curious to peek inside and see how it has changed since I saw it almost two decades ago. If I can turn the creepy garden maze into a beautiful outdoor entertaining space, will it convince the network to bring me back on for guest appearances? Or better yet, can it be trimmed and whipped into shape enough to host a fancy garden party where I can help myself fit in with the people who still judge me from so long ago?

Of course, my real goal for Thorn House is to rent it out as a vacation home and use those funds to pay for Zyra's dream college. How else will I afford Harvard University's tuition? I'm not like the wealthy residents of Thorn House Road.

My mind flicks to the guy in the flannel who smiled at me from the back row at the HOA meeting. He didn't act like the other snobs in the neighborhood. In fact, I enjoyed chatting with him and I can see us enjoying jokes over a nice dinner someday. None of my relationships stick, though, and I don't have any intention of dating until Zyra is grown and gone.

I tiptoe into the maze, taking care to make sure I can still see the opening.

After a few steps, I check my view of it, just in case. I shine my phone's flashlight behind me.

Squinting, I spy the opening. "I can just make out the escape route," I say to reassure myself, then I snort at the thought of making out. The long corridor of tall plants reminds me of the times Caspian and I snuck in here to do plenty of *making out* during the fall of our senior year.

I replace the memory with ideas for the hedges. An Alice in Wonderland-inspired design can give this yard a new life while honoring its original style.

Garden party or not, I like the idea of this challenge, something new and fresh and different from crown moldings and paint colors. Besides, it'll help me fit in with the flower and plant enthusiasts on Thorn House Road, something which this neighborhood has in abundance.

I brush my fingers against the hedges and a sharp branch scratches my wrist. I yelp and yank my arm back.

"Rude," I say. "Just like the guy who left it to me. Dem you, Caspian!" I shake my fist and curse into the silent night.

A not-so-silent voice grunts back at me.

Goosebumps raise on the back of my neck.

"Time to go," I say, hoping the sound of my voice will comfort me. I shuffle toward the exit, dipping and dodging out of the way of branches that reach into the maze's walkway.

"Does the carpet match?" someone says.

I want to run, but my feet do the opposite. I'm never good at obeying, and apparently, my body isn't either.

A chill passes through me and my heart stops, if only for a second. The skipped heartbeat reminds me I'm not the brave person I like to think I am.

Standing before me is a face so familiar it almost comforts me.

So familiar, so handsome, and so...see-through. I gulp and my eyes bug at the sight of my dead ex-boyfriend blocking the hedge maze's exit.

Maybe the walnut banister isn't my new home's biggest problem.

2
AT THE MEETING WITH A PLAN

I twist a curl of hair around my finger, resurfacing an old habit I once started as flirtation. Now, anxiety is to blame. Or maybe I can't help but play with my hair because of the familiar joke that unearthed a hundred feelings at the sight of the man I first loved.

"The carpet does not match the drapes," I respond to his silly, and slightly crude, question in a whisper.

I'm talking to myself by repeating the first words I said to Caspian Blanc a decade and a half ago in high school. Back then, the joke referred to the blue dye in my hair and was inspired by a lewd dare from other teen boys.

That moment is in the distant past—as is Caspian himself. He'd since asked another woman to marry him and then passed away, which means there's no way he's standing in front of me and raking his sienna eyes over my body now. The infuriatingly handsome smirk must be a figment of my imagination. His gray T-shirt sleeves don't hug thick arms because none of this is real. *It can't be.*

"This is not a drill," he says with a cheesy grin. It's the same response he gave me all those years ago in the halls of our high school. Except for then, he held an actual power drill in his hand as he stood in the middle of our woodshop class. If memory serves right, he revved the tool's power twice and I may or may not have *called* him a tool.

That's all this is, a memory. Except he's missing one thing...

"You don't have a drill." The awkward observation slips from my mouth. Forget the absence of a power tool, I'm talking to a person with the absence of a body.

Caspian shrugs. "No, but I have another tool."

He always met my inappropriate jokes with plenty of his own, and I fell hard. But this comment is new, not a replay of a memory from my own mind—which means, it's impossible. My brain must have conjured this new response all on its own. Right?

I frown. I've fully slipped into the delusion now and it's time I get some shut-eye.

"Okay, toodles," I say as I suck in a sharp breath. With all the courage—or denial—in the world, I step forward through the imaginary friend my tired brain has conjured.

An icy chill passes through me, raising every hair on my body from my arms to the stubborn fuzz on my upper lip. I push through the feeling. The wet grass sloshes beneath the Crocs I borrowed from Zyra. Cool water slips through the shoes' impractical holes and soaks my socks. At least that explained the sudden chill causing me to shiver.

"What?" he asks. "No comeback to put me in my place?"

I freeze halfway to the back deck and turn.

"Yep, he's still there," I say with an exhale. I swipe my palms over my eyes but it doesn't make the vision go away.

Caspian is as captivating as ever, but his confidence is gone. In its place is a twinge of fear, like the look in his eyes when I insisted we tell his family about our baby. He met the announcement of my pregnancy with excitement until his crazy family and their wealthy-people expectations came into play. I wasn't good enough for them.

Now, he stands as a wisp in the wind at the edge of the hedge maze. He's fainter than when I stood near him in the maze. His frame is gray, rather than the original bright white, and it's harder to see the definition of his chin.

"Hey, I know this is weird but don't leave yet," he says. Or rather, I imagine he says.

I take another step back and he fades more, blending into the branches and the leaves behind him.

"I know the house is a disaster, but it's a home for you and Zyra..." His voice is distant, as if it's in my head and not an actual sound.

With another step away, I can barely see what I thought I saw.

I slap my hand to my chest and take a cleansing breath. "I knew it, ghosts aren't real."

As I hurry into the house, I say it a few more times. I say it once more that night as I snuggle back into bed and pull the blanket over my head.

The next day, I repeat the phrase in the light of day where other people—real, living people—can hear me at the HOA meeting. Sunlight streams through the bay windows in the fancy sitting room at the HOA president's house.

"Everyone says Thorn House is haunted," says Darla Prune, an older woman who sits in the front row of cushioned chairs and couches.

Apparently, the HOA president moved furniture for

every meeting, transforming her sitting room into a miniature town hall, but with more expensive chairs, decor, and refreshments.

After a terrible night's sleep, and an afternoon of redesign plans, I find myself in a chair next to Zyra, defending Thorn House. Why the HOA called a second meeting in a week's time, I didn't know. Until they mentioned my house, that is.

"Ghosts aren't real," I say. I'm determined to prove it. If ghosts aren't real, bravery isn't required and I don't want my daughter to see how much of a wimp I really am. So here I am, facing the judgmental expressions of Thorn House's neighbors to defend our new home and my ticket to the cash I need.

A dozen pairs of eyes judge me as I stand in front of the cushioned folding chair and address the members of the Homeowners' Association.

"Okay." The HOA president draws out the vowels in the word. She blinks rapidly before raising her brow where her fake eyelashes reach. "Nobody said anything about ghosts."

"But Darla called it haunted," I say, with my finger pointed at the white-haired, poodle-hugging lady in the front row of chairs. Darla fluffs her short, stark curls and shrugs. Despite her disinterested behavior, I continue. "Haunted suggests there are ghosts, but ghosts aren't real. I mean, I don't think so. Who has ever actually seen a ghost? Not me." A nervous laugh escapes me as memories of last night's sighting pop into my mind's eye.

Be brave for you daughter, Olive. You can do it. I remind myself I'm not here to debate the existence of the paranormal, but to get approval for renovations that will raise Thorn House's value enough to cover college costs.

Zyra takes a break from studying the physics textbook

in her lap. She looks up at me and tugs at the end of my jean button-up that I wear open over a white tank.

"Mom, sit down," she says in her level-headed tone. My daughter knows me well enough to know I'm about to word vomit and embarrass myself in front of the entire neighborhood. Thankfully, she's my voice of reason, the angel on my shoulder and best friend who keeps me in check. She offers me a grape on a toothpick from the fancy lunch she packed. "Have a snack."

The guy in the flannel—today it's a blue and red checkered pattern—stifles a chuckle with his hand over his mouth. The way his thick, sandy hair is parted with a slight bang that hangs over to one side reminds me of a TV actor I had a crush on years ago. I can't put my finger on which one. Richard Gere? No, too old.

I shoot the guy a glare for laughing at me. He seems to understand because he mouths an apology to me as if we're old friends. Except the guy in the farmer's clothes is one of the only people in this room I'm not distantly acquainted with from my past. Almost everyone else came with recognizable names, and some are people who graduated the same year as Caspian and me.

Thoughts of Caspian remind me of last night's hallucination again, and a shiver has me copying the constant shaking of the tiny dog in Darla's arms.

Darla strokes the teacup pup's head and clucks her tongue. "I meant, the kids call it haunted and the adults call it hideous."

I take the grape and pop it into my mouth, munching as I look back and forth between neighbors. The snack stops me from saying something stupid.

The grumpiest of neighbors, Oscar, leans forward in his chair beside Darla. The soft glow from the light above shines against his bald head. "The point is, Thorn House has a bad reputation that's tanking everyone's property values—"

"Forget property values!" Kaley, the resident lawyer and school president from my graduating class, says. Her sharp, manicured fingernail jabs a stack of papers in her lap. "The facts are, we have the vote, we have the documents, and we have the power to remove the problem. What are we waiting for?"

The conversation is getting away from me. I've lost their attention, which should make me rejoice that I'm no longer embarrassing myself with ghost-talk. But it's my life's purpose to save homes like Thorn House. And the fact that it belonged to Zyra's father means we should keep it in the family.

"Thorn House is a danger," Kaley continues, and those around her murmur in agreement.

A guy I vaguely recall from my Alma Mater sits in the chair beside where she stands. I realize it's her husband, and I recognize him from his viral social media accounts as a yoga and vegan influencer. He doesn't match his wife's professional aesthetic as he sports a tank top with the name of his YouTube channel across the front. He sinks into a slouch and squints up at his wife who continues her rant.

"How many high schoolers have gotten lost in that maze?" she asks. "It nearly gave Jeanie a heart attack when her daughter disappeared."

Jeanie nods, eyes bugged as if they'll pop out of her head. "There's no cell reception out there. And let's end the rumor right now," she says in a deep southern accent. I didn't notice Jeanie before. Now I realize she and her pudgy husband are not people from my childhood, but newer neighborhood residents. She twists in her chair to face the room. Her updo reminds me of a beehive on top of her head —maybe a flaming beehive since her hair is bright red. "My daughter was not sneaking around with a boy. She's not a troublemaker. I know because she's always studying and gets straight A's for her beauty pageant reputation."

"And yet my mom worries I study too much," Zyra mutters.

I shrug. "I just don't want you to take life too seriously. And I don't worry, I always cheer you on," I whisper back to her and then hold out my hand. "Cheese me."

She slaps a slice of pepper jack in my palm from her snack.

The guy in the flannel snorts, trying to stifle it by curling his lips under. In the sea of attacks on Thorn House, he doesn't join in. For a dude who's known to be serious and keep to himself—according to Darla, who gossiped about him before he arrived at tonight's meeting—he sure laughs a lot.

"Listen," Kaley says, standing now with the stack of papers between her palms as if she'll swear on her bible of contracts to tell nothing but the truth. "We're on a timeline. I've secured a contractor to build an event center on Thorn House's property. We can begin demolition the moment we win the title of the property."

Finally, I find my voice again. "Get the...what?" I rack my brain and try to remember if this is legally possible, or merely a threat. "What about the curious dilemma of the two ladies who live there?" I point at myself and Zyra. "You can't just take our house."

Kaley purses her lips into a fake, apologetic smile. "Actually." She seethes. "We can. Thorn House has racked up fines in the past for breaking many HOA rules. Nobody was around to pay them, so we stopped trying. But now that you're here..."

She repeats the tight smile with the added effect of a wrinkled nose. "The fines have become quite large. If we sue you for the title of the property, and we will—" she glances at the HOA president who purses her lips. "I have no doubt we'll win."

Sue me? This house is supposed to save us, not drain us. My mouth falls open. It's as if I'm staring at a ghost again. Instead, it's just the pale, pinched face of my new arch-nemesis. Well, she, and the HOA president, who nods along with everything Kaley says.

I groan. I think I prefer the ghost.

"But I can't..." my voice trails before I confess my dismal financial status after being dropped by the home improvement network. "What rules is it breaking?"

Alessandra, the HOA president laughs. "What isn't it breaking? Landscaping, the house itself doesn't match the design of the rest in the neighborhood, noise complaints—"

"Okay, okay," I say, raising my hands in surrender. "Wait, noise complaints?"

She waves the question away. "You have until the end of the month to pay them or we'll see you in court. We need this event center ready for my wedding."

Kaley's jaw drops and she whips her head to stare at Alessandra. Her prim but perky blonde ponytail nearly whacks her in the eye. "Your wedding? You didn't tell me you're engaged."

With a lazy wave of her hand, Alessandra brushes off the comment. "I don't tell you everything." And then to me, she fixes her gaze and raises her voice. "We'll need you out in time to get the event center built."

I need to think of something, fast. I'm creative, I can do this. My fingers tap against the top of the folding chair in front of me and the elderly man sitting in it squints up at me.

Everybody nods in agreement and begins standing. They mingle and shuffle as if the meeting is over, but I haven't moved.

"Event center, huh?" I mumble.

Zyra glances up at me. "Please tell me you're not thinking what I'm thinking."

My shoulders drop. "What? I can be a hostess. I host things. This might be the new adventure I've been dying for."

When my daughter smirks, everything suddenly fits smoothly in my mind like a well-cut key into its lock. I know that look; she's challenging me because she knows if she doesn't, I'll go back to my comfort zone of crown moldings and carpet textures.

"You *are* stellar at running a crew," she says, referring to the tight ship I kept as captain of the home improvement show.

Time slips away as the HOA members mingle toward the exit. It's now or never.

"Wait," I say. "I have an idea." Nobody hears. Maybe *I'm* the ghost.

"Never known you to be a quiet one," Zyra says without looking up from her textbook this time. It's for Honors Chemistry, of course, since she's gunning for a career in forensic science and she's been planning her future since before she could read—the opposite of me, considering I'm still playing with career choices at thirty-three years old. She plucks a cracker from the mini charcuterie board she packed into a glass container and then pops it into her mouth.

She's right. I hop up on the cushioned seat of the folding chair and shake the curls from my face.

"Excuse me!" I shout.

All eyes are on me again. They've never dealt with the famous Olive Glass. Not since I've grown up, anyway.

"I have a proposition. What if I can fix up Thorn House into the event center you want?"

The president blinks her long lashes and Kaley folds her arms, but nobody rejects the idea, yet.

"Yeah, like, I can host graduations and baby showers, and—" I snap my fingers at the president but she doesn't like it. She raises her brows as if to challenge me in a fight. "And even weddings! We can all come to an agreement and give it a new, better reputation."

Kaley scoffs and opens her mouth to protest, but the president beats her to the punch. To my surprise, it isn't a real punch. The lawyer looks ready to hit someone.

Alessandra's lashes bunch as she squints and crosses her arms. "A new reputation? I'm listening."

"I know Thorn House comes with its baggage," I say, swallowing the lump of pride in my throat. It hits too close to home with the suitcases of drama from my personal life. "But I believe we can wipe that reputation and create new memories without having to destroy the original structure." The phrasing comes from the home improvement show as a line I've said many times. Thankfully, it's true, and Alessandra recognizes this.

False lashes dip as she narrows her eyes and nods. "That'd certainly be simpler than going to court and tearing it down."

"Yes! And I'll be doing all the work to renovate." My chest flutters with excitement. I'm not a hero in the traditional sense, but I'm certainly battling a villain.

Kaley shakes her head while Alessandra smiles. Both wield great power over me but I'm the one with great responsibility. Thorn House is the only piece of Zyra's father I have left and it will fund her college education if it kills me. And it might, considering she plans to apply to Harvard and Yale.

"I'll keep its historical style and bring the fixtures up to date," I say, confident now that the president is leaning to my side. "You won't have to hire and pay for a crew to run the event center, because I'll be doing it on my own dime." And hopefully *making* a dime, or two...thousand.

Alessandra is joined by a few other nodding heads. They're not only listening, they're agreeing, and giddiness bubbles up inside of me.

"Okay," she says. "You have one month to clean it up and, if it passes our approval, I'll waive the fines. Provided you pay the HOA dues from here on out."

"One month." I give her an awkward double thumbs up. Am I really doing this? Can I run an event center and host weddings with bridezillas and catering chaos? The idea of decorating for events, running a new crew, and envisioning big change nearly has me jumping up and down. No lives are saved, but a house is, and that's good enough for me.

"I'll even throw an approval party for the HOA!" I blurt.

Alessandra arches a carefully drawn eyebrow.

"A—uh, a garden party? That way I can show you how the maze can be a feature," I say as the puzzle forms a picture in my mind's eye. I can see it now, the maze trimmed and advertised as a courtyard. If I can prove its existence as a unique feature for fancy events, I'll save a lot of money and stick with the property's original style.

"A feature?" Alessandra hums her approval.

"What's Thorn House without a few plants?" I say.

"With the gates removed and a little trim, it'll look like a courtyard right out of a Jane Austen novel. Classy, elegant, and aristocratic." I throw around a few descriptive words that basically mean the same thing to sway their teetering votes.

"Alessandra, you can't seriously—" Kaley starts but stops when the president abandons her.

Alessandra marches across the room and juts out her hand. Manicured fingernails are pointed like weapons at my torso, ready to gut me. The smile and brightness in Alessandra's green eyes give me a little relief, but I'm still stunted, unsure of what to do with the offer.

Zyra pokes the back of my calf with her pencil and then nods toward the president's hand. I take it and give it a firm shake, a solid sign of agreement in front of the entire HOA.

"Good luck," Alessandra says, before leading the crowd of murmuring residents out of the clubhouse.

I don't hop off the chair until the door shuts behind her. When I step down, Zyra meets me, standing and tucking her textbook under her arm.

"I did it," I say in disbelief. "I won!" My voice drops to a conspiratorial quiet as I lean closer to her. "Thanks for making me read all those classic novels to you when you were a munchkin. My fancy vocabulary really seemed to push them over the edge."

Zyra laughs. After she offers me a knuckle bump for victory, she cocks her head. "Exactly how do you plan to run an event center when you've never so much as hosted a pizza party?"

"Hey, we have a *lot* of pizza parties."

"Yeah, you, me, and the homemade dough I've perfected for study nights with my friends."

I roll my eyes. "Book clubs are parties too. Just let me celebrate for a second before you get all rational."

She throws her thin arm around my neck and leads me toward the door. "Oh, there will be lots of celebrations and you better let me do the food."

I give her two thumbs up. *If this works.* Unfortunately, I don't have the first clue how to host professional events. I'll worry about that when it gets here. First, all I have to do is what I do best—design and save another lost house.

Simple as that. I've returned to the place I ran from and I'm not letting a snooty HOA president or a ghost scare me away now. Not with the ticket to my daughter's college education at the top of the hill on Thorn House Road.

I'm almost excited for the challenge because at least it'll get my mind off haunting ex-boyfriends.

3
BEFORE THE GATHERING WITH A GHOST

The house's guts didn't take long to whip into shape. Four weeks of scooping out the insides, from the hideous curtains to the cracked hardware, has me sore but satisfied. I wipe my sweaty hands on my pants and head for the front door. The old iron key that belongs to the maze's gate clinks on the carabiner attached to my belt loop. I found it behind the mantel when I demolished the ugly wood. I guess it must have slipped from someone's pocket when they built the mantel years ago.

The painting of Caspian and his judgmental parents was the first thing to go after the mantel. Somehow, I still feel their gaze. Or maybe my nerves are raw because today's party invites critics into the home and project I've grown to love. The people of Thorn House Road are mirrors of the man and woman who raised Caspian and rejected me: wealthy, prideful, and old-fashioned.

I shake it off and yank the door open. The time has arrived for me to admire the magic that took Thorn House from pumpkin to royal carriage. I'm delighted with the result, even if I didn't get the guy I hired to remove the giant fence scheduled in time.

After several steps away from the greeting mat, I sigh and fold my arms. With the skillful addition of fresh coats of paint, thrift store rugs, and hours upon hours of weeding the yard, the entire property has become a beacon of beauty in a neighborhood of cookie-cutter houses. I may have had to purchase ridiculous amounts of fertilizer to get the patchy grass to fill, but it was worth it. Thankfully, I found a steal of a deal from a guy on Facebook trying to get rid of a ton of commercial-grade fertilizer. The heavy-grade stuff worked well enough to sprout fresh greens and draw the eye from the deck I didn't have time to demo.

Yes, the yard looks amazing. What would the producers at Rose and Hose Renovation say if they saw me now? Would I get my spot back on the network? It doesn't matter, I'm ready for this new project—I think.

I grin and glance around for anyone to share in my success, but Zyra has gone back inside, and this isn't like the set of the TV show where I was surrounded by cast and crew. I don't see the face of the man I dated all those years ago, either. Caspian is nowhere to be seen and my heart sinks a little. Ghosts are spooky, and I don't want anyone to call Thorn House haunted, but it was nice to see his face again. Real or not.

I shrug and speak out loud, anyway. "This beauty is what happens after years of working within the crappy budget the channel gave me. Professional decorating for a steal." A little laugh escapes me and I gently kick at a thick patch of spongy grass.

Am I seriously trying to impress a ghost? I shake my head and walk to the backyard where the scent of blooming roses greets me. Caspian's not here, but the swing that hangs from the large oak on the edge of the maze is swaying back and forth...and there's no breeze.

"Are you here?" I ask. A mixture of hope and fear swirls in my gut with the glass of wine I downed to ease my pre-party butterflies—the kind that metamorphose from the larva of excitement. If he doesn't respond, maybe I'm in the clear, and my first experience as a hostess won't involve a haunting. But if he doesn't respond, it means I'll never see him again. Our run-in from weeks ago will become a distant memory of a silly dream. Funny how I wasn't ready to see him, and simultaneously not ready to forget about him.

"Talking to yourself again?" A cheerful voice says.

I spin around to see Zyra stepping through the Dutch door. The top half of the door has been left open to bring the natural floral scent of the garden inside. The lack of a breeze is nature's way of giving me the middle finger. At least wind won't disrupt the party if it stays this calm.

"Nope," I say. "Just practicing my lines."

She furrows her brows. "This isn't the network anymore."

With a hop, skip, and a jump, I'm at the wrought-iron table in the grass. Finding the table in the garage saved a heap of my budget and did wonders to tone down the creepiness of the iron fence. While the fence is black, ten feet tall, and twisted with ornate curves and pointed spires, the table and chairs are simple with the light look of a Parisian cafe. The wrought iron of each complements one another, at least until I can get the fence removed.

Piles of fairy lights, Mason jars, lace tablecloths, and napkins bury the table. I shove the lace into a chair to clear a space for the load in Zyra's arms. She carries two lanterns in each hand and a candle lighter under her arm.

"Network or not, everything I do will be on display for many to judge," I say, one finger in the air. I take two lanterns from her and head for the maze's ominous gate.

"You know," she says as she follows, "instead of decorating the gate, you could just lock it. It's way too high for anyone to climb. That'd keep out kids, and we wouldn't have to waste all our fairy strands to light the maze."

I throw a laugh over my shoulder. "And look like I'm hiding something from the Queen Bee and her bestie? Not a chance." I arch my feet and reach for a curved section of the gate that looks like a hand. I hook the handle of the lantern onto it. "The fairy lights will make the front pathway glow and nobody will dare go beyond that. Especially if we're busy loading them up with champagne, cheese, and my secret weapon."

"Conversation?"

I pause my inspection of the lantern's placement to give her a cheeky grin. "You know me so well."

Zyra blows a lock of hair from her face and squints at the lantern.

"Anyway," I say, "with my luck, I'd lock someone inside." I fold my arms and frown at the lantern. It sticks out awkwardly rather than the effortless look of the glowing decoration I pictured. "That looks like poop."

"Poop on a spooky gate," Zyra agrees.

I unhook it and try it on a pointed spire that looks like a spear until I realize the spire is broken and will snap off from the weight of the lantern. No matter what I do, the gate is ominous—too tall, too dark and twisty, and too suggestive of secrets when it's locked. We need to find a way to keep it from swinging shut in case of a breeze.

"You know, your dad used to call the fence a plant prison," I say with a laugh. It quickly dissipates like Caspian did the further I walked from the maze that day. "He hated this fence. He said the shadows it cast scared him when he was a kid."

"I don't blame him." She nods. "And you're right, the maze definitely needs the fairy lights."

I hum and hook the lantern back to its original spot for now. I follow her back to the table where we gather tangled strands in our arms. With as many as we can carry, we march across the lawn.

Moist grass squelches beneath my feet. We make our way toward the maze, and I want to turn and run. If I just imagine the dozens of people who will staff Thorn House Events Center, the spookiness dissipates for a moment.

The maze doesn't have the right to be this daunting in the middle of the morning when the sun is threatening to give me pit stains. I follow Zyra into the maze as I wave my arms like chicken wings. Focusing on airing out my armpits does wonders to distract me from the chill as I cross through the open gate.

I swear it drops twenty, maybe twenty-five degrees, between the hedges. The shade isn't enough to account for the drastic temperature change that takes me from worrying about wet marks under my arms to wishing I brought a jacket.

Zyra keeps talking and smiling as we walk deeper into the hedge hallways. "I've loaded each strand with fresh batteries. They should last the party in case anyone decides to explore the maze. Hopefully, the food and cocktails will keep them in the yard, at least for this event." She took her role with the menu seriously, nearly outshining my decorations. Together, we make the perfect hostess team. And while I want to be brave for her, she's the one who is undaunted by the shadows and chill of the maze.

"Ooh!" I raise my hand. "What if in the future, we advertise the maze as a bachelor and bachelorette party game?" I change my voice to sound like I'm speaking to a screen in a commercial. "Get drunk on champagne and try to find your way out. The smartest guy gets the bride!"

Zyra only shakes her head and continues around a corner.

I hurry to follow but the chill prickles my neck again and I freeze.

"Oliveyou," Caspian's voice whispers the nickname he called me all those years ago.

"You're not real," I mutter. I shuffle ahead to find another long hallway with Zyra at the end of it.

"Olive, come back," he says.

Don't look back, don't look back. I look back. *Dem you, Olive!* Not only is facing a ghost scary, but I know seeing him will spark an ache in my heart all over again.

Nobody is there, not even my baby daddy's apparition. I choose to believe it's all in my head even though I know I saw him. We spoke, and he's real despite how much I deny it. But I can't deal with the HOA president, tackle this exciting new life as an event hostess, *and* learn about ghosts.

"Maybe we should turn back before we get lost," I say. Zyra pauses and takes two steps backward, complete with the mimic of a car's beeping sound.

"That's what I wanted to suggest next," she says. "We need to go through the whole maze and make a map of it so nobody ever gets lost and we know where everything is. Also, I can't believe you only paid for someone to trim the first section. We need to clear out the overgrown branches before the next event. Then I can go back to focusing on food."

"Right. Got it."

"Is that her?" Caspian's breath is on my neck now.

I spin around, heart pounding. He's there, a faint wisp in the daylight. His shape dissipates when Zyra walks right through him. It's clear she can't see him—he's only haunting me. Does that mean he has unfinished business with me, and only me? Thoughts of our break-up come to mind. What if he never got over me? What if he hates me and it will be my doom? Not that he ever acted as though he hated me, but I'm not one to presume I know how the spirits of the dead think.

Zyra waves her hands, enthusiastic that the conversation has shifted back to food. "I think we can do real charcuterie boards for the next event if we trim the rest of these bushes ourselves rather than hire someone." She continues talking as if her father isn't right there.

The shape of his body forms again, and I notice his furrowed brow. His eyes are wet with tears but a smile pulls at his mouth.

"She's perfect," he says. "She looks just like you."

"Except for the cheekbones," I say. My round face didn't show a single angle or bone.

"What'd you say?" Zyra stops walking and waits for me to speak louder.

"Except for the cheekbones!" I shout ahead to her and then palm the space between my eyes. A raspberry sound escapes my lips.

"Smooth," Caspian says. His sad smile turns to a smirk.

"Shut up. You're not the one seeing ghosts," I whisper.

"Because being a ghost is so much better." His sarcasm always rivaled mine—the only guy who has ever kept up with me.

"You're not real," I say, hoping this ghost issue will

resolve itself before the guests arrive. It's the last thing I say before I jog around the corner. Something catches on my shoe and I stumble. I curse and glance at a small pair of gardening shears left on the ground.

Zyra picks her way to the entrance through overgrown branches. "Cheekbones?" she asks. "That's not how to pronounce it. Char-cute-rie," she says slowly. "Say it with me and you'll get it right. Anyway, I'm thinking we can use the other side of the yard to plant a garden so that all the vegetables I use for a spread will be fresh and seasonal."

"Totally," I say as I finally catch up with her. The chill fades away as we cross through the open gate. "I was just testing you. I wanted to see if you knew how to pronounce it. It's kind of like Acai berry." I purposefully say it like Chai tea and try to laugh, but sadness washes over me. Caspian felt and sounded so real, I almost miss him all over again. His mysterious death after we'd cut ties didn't give me the chance for real closure.

The sight of his face surfaced a collection of memories and feelings—a collection I wanted to bury away as much as the photographic evidence of me in low-rise flared jeans from the nineties.

We hike across the open grass. While she talks about pairing an iced tea with a buttery lobster for the HOA president's summer wedding, I twist my neck to look back.

Caspian stands at the gate, and it's now I realize there's blood on the side of his head.

4
AT THE PARTY WITH THE PRESIDENT

Fairy lights twinkle at the maze's entrance for an ethereal look. It matches the delicate cream lace and burlap theme we selected. The closer I make the garden party resemble a wedding, the more likely I am to convince the HOA to let me host events and keep Thorn House.

I hurry around the yard, double-checking the decorations and confirming the tools are stored out of sight. Earlier, I dragged the leftover giant bags of fertilizer, the shovel, gardening gloves, and trash bags full of weeds around to the other side of the house and covered them with a green tarp. Now it's time for the finishing touches, which include clearing out a few leaves blown into the yard from the maze and wiping the sweat off of the drink dispensers.

After polishing the details, I pause and scan the yard for any other imperfections. The broken spire on the gate still hangs limply, but it's too far up for me to reach it. Other than that, I'm satisfied with how everything looks.

Two giant barrels hold up a wooden plank I saved from

the demolition of the hideous mantel. On top sits three glass beverage dispensers of different shapes and sizes that we scored at a thrift shop. Zyra filled the inside with sparkling apple juice, water with freshly cut strawberries, and then she saved the third for me to add sangria.

An old wheelbarrow filled with ice and bottles sits near the iron table. I peer inside to be sure the ice isn't melting too quickly. A chalkboard sign hangs from the front. *Wheel-beer-ow* is scrawled in white with fancy looping letters I learned how to do from a YouTube video on calligraphy. I give the wheelbarrow's splintery handle a satisfying pat and move on to the food.

Tea candles in Mason jars line the center of the table. Each flickers with a warm yellow flame from the breeze that has finally arrived. Enormous platters of grapes, sliced cheeses, and round crackers are scattered artfully along the lace table runner, alternating with the jars. A small ice cream cake decorated by Zyra is the centerpiece. I adjust the large, shiny cake knife so that it's tucked under the rim of the cake plate.

The gentle wind ripples the maze and inspires thousands of clapping leaves like the sound of ocean waves. If the sway of the tall bushes didn't cast long, reaching shadows, I might enjoy the calming white noise. The rustling dies away, leaving only sporadic creaking from crickets and a distant voice.

I suck in a breath and look at the maze's entrance. A large black speaker on wheels sits to the left of the gate to signal the boundaries of the party zone. It's connected to my phone and will soon serenade guests with smooth jazz. I've spruced it up by burying the ugly black box in the rose bushes that line the outside of the fence. To the right of the speaker sits a large wooden crate that props the gate open.

Since the gate swings shut and locks automatically, we've blocked it with the heavy crate.

Zyra filled the crate with cut eucalyptus branches. I may or may not have climbed a tree on flannel guy's property and cut a few branches for its calming, fragrant scent. For my sake, I kept that detail from Zyra before she sent me marching back to his doorstep to apologize.

I shift my gaze from the blue-green leaves to the shape of broad shoulders. Caspian materializes inside the open gate. His pale frame turns to face me and he gives me a small wave, not unlike the discreet greeting he used to welcome me with when I was the new girl in high school.

Heat rises to my cheeks the same way it did back then and I bite back a goofy grin. The cool grass tickles my feet through the openings of my Saltwater sandals. I shuffle across the lawn, close enough to smell the eucalyptus.

"So, I noticed the guy I hired to do the gardening and the rowdy teens who sneak in here to make out don't mention any ghosts. Why am I the only one who can see you?" I ask, finally in the right mind to dig for answers. As if I'm a teenager trying to flirt with my crush again, I awkwardly toy with the gate's oversized key that hangs on a carabiner attached to my belt loop.

Caspian furrows his brow, creating a long crease that dips down toward the tear duct of his left eye. I remember the scar from when he fell off a trampoline in a neighbor's yard. I once convinced him to sneak into the Henderson's backyard for a joy jump, but it ended in chaos when he fell and hit the fence.

"I think it's because you called me by name," he says. The scar stretches when he lifts his eyebrows. I always told him, *I like it; the look is rugged.* "You said my name while inside the maze, and somehow I found my voice. And then I could see my hands."

"Why are you here, haunting this place?" I ask.

Darkness flickers in his eyes and my heart races. He opens his mouth to respond but a shout interrupts him.

"Mom, they're here!"

I turn to see my daughter—our daughter—leading Darla, Kaley, and Kaley's husband, Scott, around the side of the house. While Darla carries her tiny, sweater-adorned pooch, Kaley carries a scowl. Kaley flicks a wisp of blonde hair and walks in small steps so that her pantsuit doesn't wrinkle. Scott follows in her wake like a cowering, but loyal, puppy wearing a suit of his own that almost matches his wife's. The boxy fabric hangs off of his lean, wiry limbs.

When they part, heading for the drink station, I see the guest of honor. Alessandra. The HOA president has arrived. Thick, faux eyelashes pinch together as she squints and shifts her gaze around the yard. Her merlot-colored maxi dress hugs plastic, expensive curves.

"Try not to spook anybody," I say. When I turn to give Caspian a cheeky smirk, only the rustle of leaves responds. He's gone, leaving behind the trace of a chill and goosebumps on my arms.

I rub my palms over my upper arms and draw in a breath. Quickly, I crouch and flick the speaker on, double-check that it reads the connection to my phone, and then crank the volume just enough that the saxophone sounds can be heard from the deck.

"Let the show begin," I say as I straighten.

And begin it does.

I whirl from the food table to the speaker to crank the jazz music and finally make a third round to the clique of women in the deck's corner. The women rave about Zyra's food. The jug of sangria and glasses of wine lubricate the stuffiest of the guests, pulling gossip from each group in hushed and conspiratorial tones.

I play the role of the cheerful hostess. It's easy because I love the energy of buzzing conversation, the twinkling lights in the dim evening, and that I get to show off my decor.

Everyone enjoys bites of cheese until Oscar points out the ice cream cake. The suggestion for dessert spreads like a yawn, and suddenly, people crowd around the table. I squeeze my way through and offer to cut everyone a slice, but the knife is MIA.

The group meanders away, impatient and uninterested in dessert. Apparently, gossip takes the cake over real sweets.

Zyra offers refills for their drinks, and it draws attention away from the dessert drama.

On my way to track down the knife, I poke myself into the circle of Kaley, Scott, Darla, Alessandra, Jeanie and her husband Frank, and finally, the flannel guy who I've since learned is named Dex. I still can't place which actor he reminds me of, but I definitely had a crush on whoever it is.

The group's conversation is lively but focused around only two people. Kaley and Alessandra seem to be the elites of the group, the ones with the most pull over the HOA since the others flock to them for questions and suggestions about yard additions or hiring a street waxer. Even at a party, they're the center of attention.

Frank raises his glass which is already half empty. The overweight, red-faced man reminds me of Santa Claus but always slightly drunk.

"So." He nods at Dex. "I heard you struck gold in the corn industry. Hit it big and retired from farming, huh? As a writer, I'd like to pick your brain about—" A hiccup interrupts him. To his wife's obvious dismay, Frank burps. At least he covers his mouth first.

Dex shoves his hands into his pockets. "We might be able to swing that. But life as a farmer isn't very interesting. I've already forgotten most of it." He forces a laugh and I arch my eyebrow. The guy is about as socially awkward as I am, except where I talk too much, he hardly offers any explanations.

Tonight, I've successfully kept my rambling, runaway mouth on a leash. So far.

When a lull in the conversation hits, Scott glances at the watch on his bony wrist and speaks up. "Who is up for a little cross-yoga tomorrow at dawn?"

Darla openly laughs, but everyone else mutters or groans, and I gather this is a regular occurrence from Scott. I heard him complain about the lack of vegan options at the beginning of the party and hope he doesn't bring it up again. I need to divert the topic before he sours the mood.

"So, can you picture a wedding here?" I ask, smiling at Alessandra. The question doesn't come out as discreetly as I intended. I blame the second glass of sangria.

The group all turn their eyes to me, except for Frank who saunters off, announcing his search for a restroom.

Alessandra sniffs and shakes curled locks of hair away from her face. When a strand sticks to her lip gloss she raises her sharp fingernails and plucks the hair from her mouth.

"I'm not so sure," she says. "Wodsworth is a selective man. And the only wedding ever held here took place in the front yard. Not this dark, back area." She swirls her hand around to gesture at the general space.

My heart sinks like the roof of a house after its first

round of demolition. It's obvious I'm not the only one upset by her words. Kaley folds her arms and Darla rakes shaking fingers through her white plumes of hair. The poodle in her arms releases a low growl and bares his teeth at the HOA president.

You and me both, pup. You and me both. I swallow a sigh and resolve to keep trying. This event center is Zyra's ticket to a fully funded college education, and the party hasn't died down yet. I have approximately two hours to change Alessandra's mind.

"And when are we going to meet this selective man?" Kaley asks. The bite in her voice exposes her irritation. I suspect she's upset her friend hasn't shared this personal information with her.

Unbothered, Alessandra shifts her green eyes toward Thorn House and scans the tall building. "I recall a promise that this would enchant us enough to erase the memories." By changing the subject, she blatantly avoids answering the question.

I try to hold a smile but my lips quiver. "This is just the beginning." Except it's not—my budget has dried up, and, other than the removal of the fence and deck, I don't have any extra changes planned.

"Hmm." She nods. "I'm struggling to picture my wedding here."

Kaley hums her agreement and shoots Scott a sharp glare until he joins her with a lackluster nod.

"I'm not a fan of the fence," the HOA president says.

"That will be removed within the week," I say, feeling the weight of the heavy iron key hanging from my belt loop.

"Hmm." Alessandra returns her attention to the bruschetta on her plate. "At least the hor d'oeuvres are delicious." With a little raise of her china dish, Alessandra ends the conversation when she takes a bite.

I swallow hard. Does that mean it's a no? I resolve to ask again later. For now, I need to attend to the speaker, which has caught static that overpowers the sound of the drifting jazz music. I march across the lawn, stomping harder than I need to, but squishing the moist grass satisfies my frustration.

Carefully, I push thorny branches from the rosebush out of my way and reach for the speaker. Up and down, I twist the dial on the big black speaker that's connected to my phone. The higher I turn the volume, the less scratchy it sounds, but it's too loud.

"Olive," a voice calls to me from the maze.

After a moment, I abandon the speaker and step through the gate. Caspian has graced me with his ghostly presence again. But like the music, he's fuzzy, and the vision of him is almost skipping, if that's possible.

I want to tell him I'm too busy to be haunted, but the twist of his mouth catches my attention. Not to mention the blood on the side of his head. I quickly avert my eyes before the sight of it makes me faint.

He's frowning and fear flashes in his dark eyes. "I remember why I'm here."

The breeze picks up again, and I hear Darla grumble about the lack of outdoor heaters. I groan and peek around the bushes to see the group has scattered. The breeze must have been stronger than I realized because it blew out most of the candles and left the yard so dark, I mostly see the shapes of my guests rather than their faces. Quickly, I turn my attention to the dead man in front of me so he can say his piece. Then I can scrounge up more lanterns.

"I was killed," he says.

Breath catches in my throat and chills crawl over my arms and down my spine.

"Murdered," he adds with a wince. "I think, until someone solves it, I'm trapped."

I open my mouth and form my tongue around the word *murder* as my brain tries to process what he said.

Before I can speak, a piercing scream splits through the static-ridden jazz tune. The cry is loud enough to echo across the property and turn my blood cold. My heart slams against my ribcage as I run from the maze.

"She's dead!" Darla shrieks.

I spin around, searching in the direction of Darla's voice. The dim glow from the awkwardly placed lantern casts a yellow tint around something in the rose bushes.

The woman and her dog stand over a lump—a lump in the shape of a body.

5
IN THE MAZE WITH A SCREAM

Bravery never felt as far away as it does now. Only one flickering candle remains lit and it floats toward me. The flame casts a spooky glow over Zyra's face as she holds it and hurries to see what everyone is squinting at. I match her urgency and step forward to meet her on the other side of Darla, where I can be sure to protect my daughter.

The poodle releases a rumbling growl at me, baring its glistening white teeth. Wet grass squelches around me as dozens of footsteps crowd in. Bodies press closer, itching to get a glimpse of the excitement.

I hold my breath as Zyra stretches her arm, and the candle casts light over the body. Shadows dance across a familiar face. A face with long, fake eyelashes. A face belonging to Alessandra.

A collective gasp echoes through the group and nearly all the women slap their palms to their chests. A few blurt phrases like 'heavens to Betsy' and 'bloody hell'. Oscar, the elderly man from the HOA meetings, performs a sign of the cross while Kaley spits out a curse. Once I can tear my eyes from Alessandra's face, Zyra and I exchange horrified glances.

The president of the Homeowners' Association is dead in my rose bushes.

Now that I'm breathing again, the spicy scent of sangria tickles my nose and I'm just grateful it's not the smell of death.

The speaker struggles to play music, scratching with static until it bursts with a renewed life. Like everyone else, I ignore it, still hovering over Alessandra's body. The wind sends a gust strong enough to toss hair across her lifeless face and tugs at her glued lashes until one peels away. It dances over her cheek like a spider until the wind carries it away into the darkness.

We stare like a crowd of gawkers gaping at the scene until a dark patch on Alessandra's maxi dress catches my eye. A wound blooms with blood right where her heart is.

My jaw hangs open and I feel unsteady. Beside me, Dex undresses. I swear my chin is on the ground with the shock of it all until I realize he's only pulling off his flannel. He crouches and gently lays the shirt over Alessandra's face and upper body. He's the only one not muttering, not gasping or clutching pearls, and with a head clear enough to give the dead some privacy and respect.

Nobody dares to speak. Or, like me, they're incapable of forming words.

Dex straightens and rakes his fingers through his hair.

"Somebody stabbed her." Darla breathes. Her poodle barks in hoarse yips and wags its scrawny tail as if death is delightful. "We should look for evidence."

How does her brain work so quickly? I don't disagree with the idea, but shock still has me frozen in place while Darla and her pooch set off on a hunt for clues. She puts the poodle on the ground, who promptly runs to do his business in the shadows by the maze.

Others disband from the circle of gawkers and begin murmuring. Some stay close, their eyes dart across the yard at one another, while the rest scan the ground, the gate, and the bushes for evidence. I'm simply stunned, unable to move or think after seeing the lifeless body.

"I've found the murder weapon!" Kaley squeals. Her voice comes from inside the maze and my heart leaps into my throat.

Is Caspian a vengeful spirit? The last I saw, he was in the maze. I've watched enough ghost-hunting shows to know they often stick around for revenge. But from what I've witnessed, my ex's spirit could barely manifest, much less wield a weapon. Not to mention the fact that he was full of jokes rather than moans.

Like a gaggle of geese, the entire group of neighbors shuffles to the right, heads bobbing and stretching to see where Kaley disappeared to. Plenty of them squawk under their breaths along the way.

Collectively, we waddle through the giant gate, dazed and confused by the murder. Or so I suspect based on how I feel. We huddle just inside the maze, and the fairy lights surround us with a cheerful twinkle that no longer fits the mood of curiosity and...killing.

Kaley points a shaking hand at the ground. The dim lights offer just enough glow to shine against a sharp metal object at her feet. I squint and make out the gardening shears I forgot to put away.

"No, that's just—" the wind cuts me off. The rustle of leaves is so loud from inside the maze that I almost expect a saltwater wave to come crashing down on us.

Instead, the giant gate creaks as the hinges shift and it

swings toward us. A gasp hiccups in my throat. I lunge forward to stop it but I'm too late and too clumsy for the heroic feat.

The slam echoes with a clang that seems to vibrate across the entire fence. Darla screams, the scary poodle screams, we all scream, and I figure it's the ice cream cake's knife that's likely the murder weapon not the gardening shears. It was missing, after all.

"We're all going to die!" Jeanie wails.

A body presses into me, and I almost whack them until I realize it's Zyra. I'm on edge, all raw nerves and a pounding heart. I wrap my arm around her shoulders and pull her close as if she's the scared little girl in a carnival's funhouse again. But we're not in a house and there's nothing fun about murder, despite the poodle's wagging tail. Everyone exchanges whispers while the dog's stubby tail repeatedly brushes my arm. We stand squished inside the maze's entrance, afraid to be too far from the group.

"The key?" Zyra says.

I cock my head. Could someone have killed Alessandra with the huge, iron key? It's possible. The thing is solid, heavy, and oddly sharp at the end.

"Do you have it?" she asks.

"Oh!" I let go of her and grab for the carabiner on my belt loop. My hand only finds jeans. After several more pats, checking my pockets, and all around my pants, panic rises in my throat.

I meet my daughter's gaze with wide eyes. "It's gone," I whisper. "It must have fallen off when I was running around."

Or someone unhooked it from my belt loop. I swallow hard.

"This is ridiculous," Kaley shouts though I'm standing right next to her. "Open the gate, Olive."

"Someone took my key." The words blurt out before I even have the guts to try pushing on the gate. Like everyone else, I'm afraid to step away from the group and be alone in the haunted maze. Safety in numbers, after all. Of course, the murderer is more dangerous than my ex's spirit, and they're part of the group.

I take a moment to twist my head and scan the faces of the HOA members. Jeanie's cheeks are red, likely from too much alcohol. The white glow from the fairy lights highlights the orange tinge of her dye job. Her husband stands beside her, the picture of peacefulness. In fact, Frank's flat lips and folded arms make him look annoyed at the inconvenience of murder—or maybe he's hiding something. The man stands a head taller than everyone else, big-boned and muscular, rivaling Oscar the war hero. The elderly man might have lost some height with age, but he's still spry and a little scary with his permanent frown. Oscar has a battle story for each scar that marks his face like tiger stripes.

Huddled up to him is Scott. Kaley's husband shares Jeanie's rosy, alcohol-influenced expression of shock and confusion. The poor guy shrinks in between Oscar and Frank. Maybe he's letting the bigger men flank him for protection—a poor decision if either of them turns out to be Alessandra's killer.

Which of them was capable of stabbing the HOA president?

"So you locked us in here?" Kaley says.

All eyes turn to me, and I swear I feel their blame burning holes through me. Maybe I can direct their laser gazes to sear through the lock on the gate. I shuffle to the side, away from her angry breathing, and raise my palms.

"No, I swear," I say.

"Is this to cover up your crime?" she asks with her arms crossed and her eyebrow peaked now. "Because we all already saw the body."

The body. She says it like Alessandra wasn't her neighbor and friend. Is Kaley the killer? Except I notice a quiver in her voice.

Darla pipes up. "Oh, honey." She shakes her head, and the poodle stretches its neck to give me a pity lick. "You *did* look a little upset when Alessandra mentioned she didn't like the fence."

The sangria seems to curdle in my stomach. I grimace and give myself a little shake. Not only did the guy haunting me just claim he was murdered, but someone died at my party... and now the guests are blaming me.

Tonight is a failure of epic proportions.

Kaley tugs the suit jacket tightly across her torso with one hand and pulls out her phone with the other. "I'm calling the police."

"Good luck," Darla mutters, and the poodle barks.

"What's that supposed to mean?" Kaley rakes her fiery gaze over Darla, ignoring the fact that the poodle bares its teeth at her. Dogs can sense evil, right? I shiver and shuffle another step away from the murderer in the pantsuit.

Darla strokes the poodle's head. "Shush now, Gassy." With a shrug, she lazily nods her head at Jeanie, who's nursing a mason jar of sangria in both hands. "It's no secret that Mini Miss Pageant came here to get necking with her boy toy because it's private. She knew phones don't work out here and her mom couldn't track her location."

Jeanie gasps and her arm shoots out. The half-glass of

sangria splashes across Darla's face, cream sweater, and white poodle. Red liquid drips from the horrified old woman's face and into her open mouth.

We match her shock with our jaws on the ground.

"How dare you?" Jeanie growls in a raspy voice. "My daughter was tutoring that young man and they needed some peace and quiet." Her voice breaks.

The large men offer Darla help. While Oscar gives her a handkerchief, Frank mouths a gentle apology before he carefully pulls his wife away from the group.

Gassy licks sangria off his owner's chin while Darla dabs at the alcohol in her eyes.

"Tutoring him in necking," she mumbles and I catch a wink from her. I trail her gaze to the two men nearby. Both Scott and Oscar smirk as if amused by Darla's innuendo.

One shock after another almost has me forgetting about the death and destruction at my garden party. I pat my pockets down again, and then squint at the grass to search for the key.

A loud clang resonates across the fence again and we all jump. I almost expect to see Scott diving into Oscar's arms, but I look to the gate instead of at the back of the crowd.

The fairy lights catch the glow of a white T-shirt pulled tightly across a muscular back. Dex fiddles with the gate's lock—again, he's the only one with any sense. Or is he guilty and trying to get out before we all realize it? My gaze lingers, for more than one reason. Though the moment of pretending my entire world isn't crashing down on top of me doesn't last.

Dex tries to reach through the gate, but his forearm is too thick to fit between the poles. His fingers manage to wrap around the lock and he picks at the device with a pocketknife.

"Let me try," I say, knowing the quirks of the old lock. "Even with the key it takes a lot of jiggling."

Dex hesitates, holding the pocketknife close to him while his ocean eyes scan me.

I lean a little closer. "I'm not the killer if that's what you're thinking. Unless we're talking about the death of this party because apparently, I slay at event planning. Wait, slaying is a good thing, isn't it? I suck at slang. I think I'm still young and then I look in the mirror and it's like, whoa, who is that old broad? You know?" I can't stop talking. My nerves do me dirty and my mouth runs like a broken toilet, always refilling until it spills crap all over the entire house. "Coming back to my Alma Mater and Thorn House Road totally tricked me into thinking I'm a teenager again. I mean, Jeanie's daughter isn't the only one who's snuck into this maze for a good ol' make-out session, if you catch my drift." An awkward laugh escapes me and I think I might wrangle control of my mouth. I don't. Filling the silence is a knee-jerk reaction, so I keep going before reason has time to shut me up. "I mean, not now. Not as an old gal. I don't make-out. I would, I was just referring to teenage me with the sneaking thing..." Finally, thankfully, my energy runs out.

Dex blinks beneath furrowed brows. Without a word, he offers me the pocketknife.

"Thanks." I hold it up and give it a little shake. I step toward the gate and dig the pointy end into the opening as if I have any clue how to pick a lock. But desperation has me convinced any action is better than standing around and allowing the pantsuit killer to accuse me of a violent crime.

"I know you didn't hurt Alessandra," he says.

My shoulders relax and then immediately tense again when I hinge on his next words.

"Because you killed her?" It slips out. I cringe. At least I'm the one holding the knife in case he decides to strike. *Please don't let the hot guy be the killer.* Of course, it's just my luck to fall for the wrong man as I did with Caspian, the wealthiest boy in town and son of a senator.

Not that I'm falling for anyone now. Unless my body falls to the ground because they've stabbed me too. But the calm, focused vibes I get from Dex don't ramp up my nerves. I can't help but notice how different he is from the rest of the residents of Thorn House Road with his disinterest in gossip, casual clothing, and genuine smile.

Dex chuckles and shakes his head. "No, because you were nowhere near her."

I breathe again. "Oh, right. That makes sense. Did you see who was?"

"No, it was too dark," he says. "But I'm willing to bet it's the same person who took your key."

I stop picking the lock to look at him. The scrape of the knife against the iron hurts my ears, so the break is a welcome one.

"So if we find the key, we find the killer," I say, getting excited about securing answers and getting the heck out of this maze.

"We?" He snaps. "What makes you say that?"

"I mean, collectively, everyone." I wave my arms around gesturing at nothing in particular.

He relaxes, and the concern on his face melts away. "No, no, *we* is good. You're the only one I can verify since you were on the other side of the yard near me. I'm going to need your help with this case."

This case? He says it as if he's an investigator. As if he's done this before. I cock my head at him and watch as he squints at the others. Dex has a secret beneath the flannel shirts and farmer's tan.

"I need your help too." A disembodied voice breathes into the wind.

Caspian manifests inside the gate where the iron poles cut right through his wispy body.

"I'm remembering pieces of the last year of my life," he says. "When you mentioned the key, it triggered a memory. Someone came after me with that key but I can't remember who, or why. Maybe it's how they killed me."

I freeze, gripping the pocketknife's with both hands like a candle. The moonlight glints off the blade and casts a flash of light across the group. One of them is guilty of not only one but maybe two murders, in this very garden.

Spooky. And here I thought tonight meant I'd only have to conjure up enough courage to face the HOA president's criticisms.

How the heck am I, an interior decorator-turned-event hostess, supposed to solve this?

6
IN THE GARDEN WITH THE KEY

Did Caspian suffer the same fate as Alessandra? Did he get stabbed with the pointy, antique key? My stomach gurgles and I realize there's no access to a bathroom inside this maze. I might pee my pants in front of the entire neighborhood and look even more guilty. And the worst part is, my daughter is trapped here too. In my quest to make her life better with this house, this party, this ticket to help her at Harvard, I've gone and gotten her stuck inside a maze with a murderer.

Zyra shuffles up to me, and Dex narrows his eyes. His gaze trails past her at the two men backed against the maze's wall of bushes, where Scott and Oscar are exchanging quiet words.

My daughter places her hand on my shoulder. "Are you okay?"

I should be asking her that. A dead body is bleeding in the middle of the party we've spent days setting up. Of course, this is her bread and butter, the type of incident that'd give her future career as a forensic scientist job security. Still, that doesn't ease my frustration. I should be brave, for her.

"Not a fan of the red," I say. With a hard swallow, I gesture at the spot on my chest where Alessandra suffered a wound. Zyra nods, likely recalling when we donated blood at her request for her fourteenth birthday and I fainted on the floor. Or any other time she's witnessed me pass out at the sight of blood.

"I'll catch you if you fall," she says, reading my mind.

"And then we'll look like partners in crime," I mutter.

Everybody murmurs and theorizes, daring to glance around their immediate areas. Not one of us is brave enough to move away from the group. So, we stand motionless, with no plan.

Zyra stops twisting purple and brown hair around her finger as she shakes her head. "No, it's the people who *don't* react to murder that look suspicious."

I meet her gaze and then look past her at Oscar, the one who didn't scream or even frown at the sight of the body. He towers over Scott who is at least six feet tall. Despite judgmental glares from every woman on Thorn House Road, Oscar had the guts to show up to a garden party in cargo pants with a green camo print and a black T-shirt. For a guy in his seventies—maybe older, nobody knows Oscar's actual age, just that he's fought in a war or two, maybe three—he's built like a tank. And which wars? He has never said, but he is always sure to drop hints about how many enemies he proudly 'took out'.

I shiver and turn my head so he doesn't catch me staring. I side-eye for a discreet visual investigation and feel like an official detective—something I'll have to be to show Kaley I didn't kill the president. With his arms crossed, Oscar's thick muscles bulge. If he were younger, with a hair or two left on his head, I suspect he'd be the type of dude who brags about bench-pressing a woman's body weight.

The fairy lights shine off of his bald head and it reminds me of a single, bare light bulb in an interrogation room. The man didn't scream or gasp when the rest of us did. I knew that much, considering his deep voice didn't bring down the high octave of our noisy shock.

And what about Frank? Jeanie's husband stands beside her, with his hand on her lower back and a pint of beer in the other. He nonchalantly takes a sip and then smacks his lips. Who behaves so chill after witnessing a murder and then becoming trapped with the killer? The only one unbothered by death is likely the one who caused it.

At least, that's what I suspect after binging hours of true crime podcasts and CSI episodes for Zyra's research. It was that or watch Bones reruns for the millionth time at her request.

I nudge Zyra with my elbow. "You're right. Thanks for making me watch those murder shows."

She rolls her eyes. "They're not murder shows, they're mysteries, and they keep your mind sharper than reality TV."

"My mind is as sharp as—" I clamp my jaw before saying *the key*. The darned thing was ancient, with a weird pointed tip that I assumed was to make it unique. Was it fashioned that way for murder? Based on Caspian's claim, I wonder if it was used to kill him. I sway at the memory of the blood on the side of his head. Despite the fact that the key didn't match his injury, its odd shape still struck me as suspicious. I drop my voice to conspiratorial tones. "We need to find that key."

"Clearly, picking the lock isn't working," Kaley says with a scoff. She tosses blonde hair over her shoulder, whips a claw clip from her clutch that matches the pinstripes of her pantsuit, and wraps her straight locks into a tight bun. "Also, our hostess is doing nothing to find this alleged key."

My jaw drops, but she's not wrong. What's clear is that I'm not a detective. Instead of investigating, I wasted time desperately picking at the lock.

Kaley tilts her chin up and to the group says, "I'm finding another way out."

"Me too!" Jeanie calls. She says it loud enough that everyone can hear she's agreed with the queen bee.

"That's not a bad idea," Zyra says to me. "I'm going to follow from the back so I can keep an eye on everyone's behavior."

Kaley spins around and marches into the shadow where the glow of the fairy lights can't reach. "Let's go."

The leaves rustle, brushing against one another like hundreds of green hands clapping for Kaley's brave announcement. I want to grab the gardening shears and snip a few of the smug bastards for cheering for my archnemesis. Long before Kaley threatened to demolish my house, she flirted with my boyfriend. Sure, it was high school, but I still remember how she tried to convince him to take her to prom.

The leaves continue clapping until the breeze dies down.

"I can still cut you down," I threaten the bushes with a whisper and a glare until I realize Caspian can hear me. Heat flushes my neck and cheeks. I'm embarrassed in front of a ghost. Apparently, dead or not, an ex-boyfriend can still trigger plenty of emotions.

The faint shape of his form stands in front of the bushes by the gate. He's halfway inside the hedges, halfway out.

"Is there a way you can unlock it?" I ask as quietly as possible. The group has turned to follow the queen bee, anyway.

Caspian shakes his head, and the heat rises again. If he can't feel the spiky branches splitting through his ghostly body, of course he can't grip the lock or key.

"But I might be able to lead you to the other exit," he says.

"There's another exit?" My heart beats faster. Kaley is onto something.

"It's long, and I can't remember all the turns, but my memory seems to come back in pieces with your help."

I cock my head like a confused puppy.

"You're the reason I'm not invisible anymore." He smiles, and it's gorgeous—ghostly, but just as gorgeous as the day I told him I was pregnant with our child. "When you called me by name, I was able to remember who I was and manifest." He looks down at himself. "Though I can't say I love that you can see through me."

I cluck my tongue. "I always could."

He drops his expression to deadpan, which matches his unalive state fairly well. "Anyway, you help me and I'll help you."

"Deal." I stick out my hand to shake on the agreement.

He stares at it for a moment and then passes his through mine. The chill of his essence sends goosebumps over my knuckles and up to my wrist and forearm.

"How about a nice nod then," I say with a flick of my eyebrows.

The curt lift of his head reminds me of the way we'd greet each other across the hall in high school. We'd share a little nod during class, or when we were busy running with different groups of friends. Back then, he always let me know he was thinking of me.

I hurry to follow the group before they turn the corner. When I jog up to Zyra, I point at the gardening shears in her back pocket and make a face.

"In case we need them," she explains. "There's no blood on them, but it doesn't mean they weren't wiped clean."

"I think the murder weapon is the key," I say. "Someone took it off of me, then stabbed Alessandra."

"And then they locked us in here," she says with a shiver.

"Bingo," I say, tapping my nose. "The key is the key to solving this. Before we know it, this murder will be a memory. I'll write a tell-all memoir so that Oprah reads it and my business becomes famous."

"Mom," Zyra chides me.

"I'm kidding, I don't have the patience to write a book." Really, I said it to ease her anxiety.

Forensic science and true crime podcasts create distance from the killer. But being locked inside of a giant maze with the murderer is another story. I don't blame her for buzzing with worry. Before a big exam or a school dance, I always calm my daughter by way of distraction. When I ramble about something off-key, she corrects me and feels a sense of control again. It always helps when she's lost rein of her nerves.

A chuckle pulls me from my thoughts.

Dex drops back while Caspian manifests on my other side. Suddenly, the little posse at the caboose grows. One moment it's just me and my daughter and the next, the two of us are joined by my ex-boyfriend, and my future ex-boyfriend.

I give myself a little shake. I'm not interested in dating,

just interested in admiring the muscles of Dex's forearms and how he snickers at the inappropriate way I deal with death. Casual conversation and jokes might make me look more guilty, but I don't know how else to handle life. When peers teased me about my pregnant belly during high school, I didn't cry, I laughed along with them and pretended to smuggle a basketball at the homecoming game. I'm older now, not as dorky—or maybe more if you ask Zyra—but the murder triggered my nerves as much as hers.

"What do you know about Jeanie Mayonnaise?" Dex asks.

"Other than that her last name is a condiment for tuna fish?" I shrug. A light bulb pops on inside my head at the memory of the sangria's scent. "Wait, she *is* fishy! Jeanie was standing to my right next to Darla when we were around Alessandra's body. I remember smelling her drink and that's where I had the key on my belt loop."

Dex nods and taps something into the notes app on his phone. "Huh. But I heard you say you think the key is the weapon, and if Jeanie used it to kill, she'd have taken it before then."

My shoulders drop. "What are you, some kind of detective?"

He widens his eyes for a second and then blinks the shock away. What is that about? I don't mean to offend. In fact, Dex's simultaneous interest in the mystery while remaining level-headed about the murder, makes him even more attractive to me.

Heat rises in my neck as I become aware of Caspian flanking my other side. His ghostly gaze shifts between me and Dex. The frown twisting his face makes him more of a spooky ghost and less the charming guy I fell for years ago.

I'm not an apparition, but my ex-boyfriend can likely see through me as easily as I can him. Is he...jealous?

Dex nods at the blonde woman marching in the front of the pack. "I asked because she's agreeing with everything Kaley says."

"I've noticed she does that a lot," Zyra says. "At the HOA meetings, I mean."

I nod. "It's true. She wants Queen Bee–uh, Kaley's approval for some reason."

"Ah," he says, "I guess I've never noticed. I thought Jeanie was the queen bee," he uses my phrase and shoots me a little smirk. "She's the one with the famous daughter, right?"

"Only if you count winning the Mini Miss America pageant as famous," I say as I step over a broken branch on the ground. We turn another corner and head deeper into the darkness of the maze. "I guess they *were* on TV."

"What about the scandal around it, though?" Dex waves his hand as if trying to recall details.

"Scandal?" Zyra and I say it at the same time.

"Jinx, you owe me a Starbucks," I say, before she can. She groans but I know it's helping keep her calm because she's no longer frowning at the two tall men. To Dex, I say, "You know something we don't."

He shakes his head at us and continues. "A while back, I, uh, questioned Alessandra about something, uh...private."

"Uh, that's, uh, suspicious," Caspian says, mimicking Dex's awkward dialogue. I go to elbow my ex but my arm passes through his ribcage. *Spooky*. At least no one else can hear Caspian's obvious accusation.

Dex continues, "she said she doesn't disclose the business of HOA members unless it's illegal. According to her, whatever Jeanie is keeping under wraps isn't interesting enough to mention."

"Ooh," I seethe. "That'd definitely piss Jeanie off. She always wants to be the center of attention."

Zyra tilts her head, considering this. "So you're saying Alessandra knew a secret about Jeanie?" Leave it to my daughter to ask the logical questions. Maybe she should become a detective rather than a forensic scientist.

Dex nods and taps his nose the same way I do. When he realizes I notice, he smirks again. We're two peas in a pod of inappropriate behavior. People shouldn't joke during a murder investigation.

"Pbbt." The ghost at my side scoffs. "Jeanie's not the only one with a secret."

I think twice before trying to elbow him this time. Instead, I shoot him an icy glare.

Caspian offers a shrug that's anything but innocent. "Listen to our daughter," he says. "She's smart enough to recognize that anyone who isn't obviously upset by the murder is a suspect." Caspian stares at Dex, clearly clueless that he just dissed me with the comment, too.

I ignore him and piece the puzzle together. "So Jeanie had motive, and means, if she's the one with the key *and* depending on when she took it. I'm not sure when it went missing."

"Don't forget her outburst," Zyra adds. "Maybe she knew you smelled her drink. By dousing, Jeanie won't be the one you remember smelling like sangria."

Color me impressed. Of course, everything my daughter does impresses me. Solving a murder will simply be another mark on her checklist of accomplishments.

I hop over a rock in the middle of the path and nearly bump into Dex. Instead, I dodge his shoulder and lose my balance. The ground comes up fast but Dex is faster. He grabs the crook of my elbow and helps me straighten.

"Good thinking," he agrees with Zyra, not missing a beat. "In the chaos and panic, it'd be easy to mix up the timeline and details like that."

I nod and the four of us, ghost included, turn our attention to the redhead in the floor-length sundress. Jeanie swings her hips as she hurries to keep her short legs moving as fast as Kaley's strides.

I mull over Jeanie's possible motives. Kaley was the closest in terms of friendship with Alessandra. Jeanie wants Kaley's attention. It makes perfect sense that Jeanie would remove Alessandra so she can be the chosen friend.

If only I could remember when the key went missing, we'd have this mystery in the bag.

"Jeanie Mayonnaise killed the president," I say under my breath, "in the garden with the key."

7
WALKING THE HALL WITH THE HAUNT

Long rows of giant bushes separate us from the rest of the world. Yet, somehow, we're right in the thick of society: a society of snobs, secrets, and one future forensic scientist. The four of us walk, or float, several paces behind the group so they don't hear our theorizing...or that I'm calling them names.

"So Jeanie's a liar and a cheater?" I say. The truth is, snobbery is just their defense, a way they define their uniqueness in a cookie-cutter street where they're all the same and yet entirely different.

Who knew the threat of being trapped with a murderer would make me philosophical? Really, it's just that I want to understand them. If I get inside Kaley or Jeanie or Oscar's heads, maybe I'll get answers.

"Jeanie's two goals in life are to impress the queen bee and win pageants vicariously," I say, guessing at my neighbor's deepest desires.

Zyra hums. "Which really means she just wants to fit in."

I smile and nod at my daughter. She's the better detective, and my heart bursts with pride. Maybe I'm not so different from Jeanie. I didn't kill Alessandra or throw my drink in Darla's face, but I understand the desire to shout your child's accomplishments from the rooftops. Or in Jeanie's case, on reality TV about pageant princesses. Of course, announcing Zyra's sleuth skills in the middle of a murder investigation might make me look guiltier. They won't believe her if they think I'm the killer.

"Don't you think she should be a detective?" I lean forward to make eye contact with Dex on the other side of Zyra. With my thumb, I motion to whom I'm referring and Zyra rolls her eyes.

His jaw shifts back and forth and his brows furrow. In a flash, his face relaxes, and he looks away. "How would I know?"

That was weird. Maybe there is something more than jealousy fueling Caspian's suspicion of Dex.

Zyra jumps in. "It's basic high school hierarchy, really. A neighborhood isn't all that different from teenage cliques. Jeanie does all of these things because she thinks she'll feel fulfilled if people like Kaley accept her." She sighs. "I see it every day between classes."

"Seriously, you guys don't even need me for this investigation," I say, only half-joking. If I can focus on the mystery surrounding Caspian, maybe he'll get his memory back quicker and we'll escape before the murderer comes for us.

Dex stops suddenly and turns to me. His arms cross his chest and he frowns. "Why do you keep referring to me as an investigator?"

I raise my hands in mock surrender. "Aren't we all detectives tonight?" A chill brushes against my ear. Finally, I realize who he reminds me of. Dex is a regular Fox Mulder from *The X-Files*, or rather, a David Duchovny lookalike. No wonder it was a crush at first sight.

"Is it just me, or is this guy acting paranoid?" Caspian whispers as if the others can hear him.

I swat at him like he's a devil on my shoulder. Funny how his ghostly figure scared me only days ago. A murder at your garden party really puts things into perspective.

I take a cue from Detective Zyra and try to observe silently as we hike. Unfortunately, Jeanie is a bore to watch and I'll find nothing suspicious or even interesting about her. She bustles to keep up with Kaley—not an easy feat in a long dress.

As we walk, I drop back and insert myself between Dex and Zyra. A chill steals down my spine and I glimpse the ghost's frown. But it's not directed at me.

Caspian scans Dex's jeans, cowboy boots, and tight T-shirt—another gutsy outfit to wear at a garden party on Thorn House Road. I'm not complaining, though. The heat of his body is nice as the breeze picks up and the night's temperature continues to drop. I don't hate being this close to Dex, but I don't love the way Caspian swallows hard. Ghosts swallow? I shake my head to stop my mind from getting sucked into a tangent about paranormal theory.

I nod at Jeanie. "She has nowhere to hide the key or any other weapon."

"Good eye," Dex says, and I swear he winks again.

"So where'd she stash it?" Zyra muses.

The three of us tilt our heads in sync to double-check that Jeanie isn't carrying a purse.

"She doesn't have it," Dex says, finally.

I cluck my tongue. "That's what you get when you don't buy dresses with pockets."

Dex quirks his eyebrow at me and suppresses a small smile. "You get proven innocent?"

"Whatever." I wave him off the same way I did Caspian's comments. "You know what I mean." I take the opportunity to rake my eyes over his back pockets that hug his lower half like a pair of well-fitted gloves. If gloves were jeans. "I guess you don't know what I mean. Look at those pants!"

Dex clears his throat and cocks his head at me. Did he catch me in the act of checking him out? In my defense, he *did* act odd both times I referred to him as a detective, so I have a real reason to keep my eye on him.

Zyra interjects with a pat of her own pants. "Before my mom launches into a two-hour rant about how women's clothes need more and bigger pockets, just know that's what she's talking about."

"Ah." Dex nods. "Admiring mine, I see."

I gawp.

Caspian scoffs. "The guy's an arrogant a—"

"My pockets," Dex says, not knowing he interrupted the ex-boyfriend haunting us. "You were admiring my pockets."

I snap my fingers and point at him. "Right. Yep. Yeah, that and just making sure you're not hiding the key."

"He's hiding *something*," Caspian growls, but it's a faint sound and I realize the further away from him I am, the less solid his frame becomes. With a hop, skip, and a jump, I return to his side. The temperature of death is cold, but I feel a familiar warmth in my chest when his hand passes through mine. Would he hold it if he could? Would we interlace our fingers the way we did when we were in love?

I glance over and see he's looking at me, maybe gauging my reaction to his touch.

I shake off the memories but I can't rid myself of the butterflies I get when we're this close.

Maybe Caspian's right, maybe I'm looking in the wrong place. Someone killed Caspian, and someone killed Alessandra. Are they connected? How many killers could there be on Thorn House Road?

"Is there anything else you remember about your death?" I whisper.

Caspian squints at the ground as we walk. "I think..." he meets my eyes and I'm lost there in the shade of dark chocolate, both alluring and comforting, like a treat with a glass of Merlot. "I think there was a woman with me when my life ended."

8

IN THE FACE WITH A PUNCH

We turn another corner that brings us to the narrowest hall of bushes yet. The tightness of the overgrown branches force us into single-file lines.

We dodge branches on the ground and duck under leaves. Kalcy hops effortlessly over the mess of plants and continues, confidently selecting one of two forks in the pathway. Since Caspian doesn't speak up, I assume it's the right direction.

The men shoulder their way through the overgrown areas. Scott grunts as the bush's poky limbs scratch at his bare elbows, and Oscar shoots him a look of furrowed brows. Apparently, Mr. War Hero is unimpressed by Scott's distaste for broken skin.

Darla sighs and slows her pace. "My dogs are barking." Her southern accent makes it sound like she's rhyming the word barking with squawking, which isn't an inaccurate description of the poodle's yips.

"It's actually the first time your dog isn't barking," Oscar grumbles, but after one glance from Darla, he takes Gassy into his thick arms. Darla didn't even ask, but he seems to have understood her expression and need for a little help.

"Thank you," she says, rubbing her shoulder. "My arthritis is flaring." She digs into her giant needlepoint purse with the shape of a black poodle on the design. After some rummaging, she produces a lace handkerchief that she uses to wipe her brow.

I crane my neck and spy something shiny in Darla's purse. Where did the killer stash the weapon? If Jeanie is the murderer, she doesn't have a purse or pockets to carry it. We need to move on to another suspect.

I lean close to Zyra and Dex again. "Jeanie's the only one we're certain has a secret that Alessandra knew."

"But nowhere to carry a weapon," Dex says as a reminder.

Zyra nods and says, "She's at the bottom of my suspect list, for now."

"That's what I'm saying." I hum in agreement. "So who do we investigate next?

Zyra's short hair brushes her shoulders as she shrugs. "In a neighborhood with this much drama, everyone's probably hiding a juicy tidbit."

I watch as the hem of Jeanie's checkered maxi dress catches on a low-hanging branch and snags. We've gone deep enough that we can't see anything beyond the walls of green. The leaves have a life of their own, rustling and brushing against us as we squeeze through. Narrow passages where the branches have had years to obscure the maze's original path make my chest tighten. I'm temporarily a claustrophobic.

"Should we stop and ask for directions?" I ask Caspian but nobody knows I'm talking to a ghost. The question is nonsense anyway, since we're all as clueless as the next person. Dex grunts a laugh at the oddity of it while everyone else ignores me.

"I never ask for directions," Caspian says, with a smug lift of his chin.

"This doesn't exactly look like a hotspot for pedestrian activity," I say, gesturing at the wild look of the bushes that haven't seen gardening shears in a decade or more. Not even the branches on the ground show signs of foot traffic. "Where do the makeout-ers go?"

The living people don't answer but my ex-boyfriend jumps on the memory of us sneaking out here.

"We would know." Caspian snorts a laugh. Though he's wrong. This isn't how I remember the maze, the place where Zyra was conceived. Something about the comment rubs me the wrong way.

He dumped me all those years ago. Even if he wants to hold my hand now, it's far too late. Right? Or am I trying to convince myself I'm over him... all over again?

"Ugh." I shake my head at my own stupid emotions and the sound escapes me.

"Fine!" Kaley halts and we all almost collide like a row of dominos.

Oscar stops just in time not to steamroll Darla, but Jeanie slams right into Kaley. The queen bee shoots Jeanie a sharp frown and then turns her wrath to me. Wisps of blonde have escaped her bun and splay around her like a frame of static-induced hair.

"Moan and groan all you want, Olive." Kaley jabs her finger in my direction. The glow of our phone flashlights illuminate her face just enough for her to remind me of a bully telling scary stories at camp. "But it won't convince me that you don't know exactly where we are right now. This is what you wanted, right? For us to be lost and away from Alessandra's body? Do you have someone stashing the evidence right now?"

Caspian's manifestation fades slightly as he points at Kaley. "I remember her," he says, breathless. "We went to school with her."

"Yeah, she was prom queen," I say as quietly as possible, but Kaley has the hearing of a cat and looks ready to scratch my eyes out.

Kaley laughs. It's a harsh sound, more of a bark than the poodle's *actual* bark. "Is that what this is? Jealousy from our teenage years?"

Unbothered by the narrow passage, Kaley shoves branches aside. Dry leaves crunch beneath her sensibly heeled shoes as she marches toward me. Even Oscar, who towers three heads taller, shuffles out of her way. Fire burns in her baby blue eyes.

"Am I next on the chopping block, Olive?" she asks.

Darla gasps and Gassy whimpers. Her poodle always seems to sense his owner's distress. If only I had an attack dog to protect me now. But I'm out of luck, and it seems, framed for Alessandra's murder. Really, whoever did it is a genius. They knew everyone heard the president deny me her approval. I look like a real jerk considering I suggested the party, invited her here, and then she got stabbed in the middle of my backyard.

Kaley stops in front of me and jabs her finger inches from my sternum. I wonder if she's second-guessing whether she can knock me over with a little push and a lot of anger. "Are you going to stab me for getting what you wanted, too?"

What the heck is she talking about?

I shake my head and take a step back. Kaley doesn't

normally intimidate me, but her outfit offers at least six places to hide the key.

"I never wanted to be prom queen," I say.

The suit coat wrinkles as she folds her arms. "Everybody might think you killed Alessandra for denying approval of Thorn House, but this crime was about Caspian wasn't it? You didn't like that he was friendly to me in high school and I'm sure you hated that Alessandra for the same reason."

"I'm lost," I admit, glancing at where the ghost stood beside me. Caspian has moved from the spot, leaving nothing but cold air behind. Alessandra wasn't from our high school or an original resident of Thorn House Road, so Kaley's comment makes no sense.

"No." She purses her lips for a moment and the harsh look ages her with lines on the skin around her mouth. "You know exactly how to get out of here, don't you? Because you've been in this maze before."

Everyone stares at me, frozen and holding a collective breath as they wait for my response. I'm aware of each of them, and what they must think of me. Frank, red-faced and swaying slightly, takes another drink of his beer. White foam lines his top lip like a mustache.

It doesn't matter what they think. I'm innocent.

"No. I mean, I'm lost about the connection between the two," I say. "What does Caspian have to do with Alessandra?"

Kaley throws her head back and laughs. "Don't play stupid. They were engaged!"

My blood turns to ice. Maybe I should look for my dead ex—the fiance to the other dead person in my yard—but I search for Zyra's face in the crowd. She's right next to me, of course, standing her ground, only breaking her glare at Kaley to look at me.

Concern wrinkles her forehead and reaches her widow's peak. The expression matches her father's face while her wide eyes mirror mine.

"No, he was going to marry someone named Alex," I say, defending myself with the little information I have about Caspian's love life. I didn't keep tabs on the details since he didn't have the guts to become part of his daughter's life. He made it clear we were meant to go our separate ways.

Spittle wets my face as Kaley laughs again. "Nobody calls her Alex anymore."

"Called," Frank says.

Kaley looks ready to throat-punch him, but he stands a few feet away with an arm around his wife's shoulders.

He raises the pint of beer and takes another sip before clarifying. "As a writer—" he huffs, interrupted by a jab from Jeanie's elbow.

"Don't make yourself look suspicious," she says. Maybe Jeanie thinks she whispers because her voice comes out raspy, but we all heard her little warning.

With a hiccup and a shrug, her husband brushes it off. "I was on the pot when the president got whacked. Everybody knows it ain't me." he says, slipping into poor grammar from the alcohol. This piece of evidence feels new but I realize it's not and that I simply forgot about him. With his reminder, I recall Frank downing a whole beer and promptly abandoning the group gossip in search of a bathroom. "I just mean," he continues, "it should be said in the past tense, 'cuz the lady's dead."

Are Alessandra and Alex really the same person? My mind reels with the information and my heart thuds against my ribcage. All this time, the HOA president was the same woman Caspian left at the altar. I never dug for details since it always made sense that Caspian ran. He never could commit to anyone, not even a girl approved by his snobby parents.

A sob escapes Kaley. Her anger cracks and sadness spills out.

"She was my friend," she says between cries.

"Her only friend," Darla says, glancing at Oscar.

Oscar raises an eyebrow. "Poor gals."

Darla nods and lifts her hand to scratch Gassy's head. Gassy is happy being held at Darla's eye level in Oscar's arms. "Mmm." She never takes her eyes off Kaley.

Zyra pulls the gardening shears out of her pocket. "Wait," she says. "This is classic misdirection. And you're a lawyer, right?" Kaley frowns but it doesn't deter Detective Zyra. She continues despite no response to her question. "You're naming pieces of truth and pinning them on my mom."

With her hands on her hips, Kaley leans closer to Zyra. "Now wait just a minute—"

Zyra interrupts and holds up the sharp tool. The curved pointed tips nearly poke Kaley in the nostrils. "And you found these."

"Which led us into the maze," I say, riffing off my daughter's train of thought.

"That's right," Dex chimes in. Carefully, his eyes rake over Kaley and I suspect he's searching for clues.

Kaley shakes her head. Blonde hair sticks to her shiny lips after she licks them. Slowly, she backs up, right into Caspian's frame and turns her attention to me. A sudden, violent shiver shakes her entire body. I suppress the gasp in my throat at the sight of him again.

Caspian's face pales, if that's even possible for a ghost. He's staring at Kaley inside of him. "She's the one who tried to get me to cheat on you in high school...and cheat on Alex, too. She wanted me to call off the wedding and run away with her—oh my gosh," he interrupts himself and frowns, gingerly brushing his fingers across his faint lips. "She tried to kiss me the night before the wedding. I remember her telling me that Alex was using me and I deserved someone more on my level, like her."

My ex-boyfriend's memories have confirmed it for me. Kaley is the killer, and she's standing right in front of me. Panic rises in my chest like a sudden bout of heartburn. I need to get out of her reach, and fast.

Before I can duck, Kaley's arm shoots out. She doesn't make contact with my throat, instead pointing at the man beside me. "He's got a gun!"

The attempt at distraction doesn't sway us from staring at her. Dex is the last person I'm afraid of right now. And it seems Kaley is full of lies, or a master of misdirection, as Zyra called it.

Dex steps up to her with his hand out to calm her. Relief floods me as he places himself between us so she can no longer reach me. Even if it's not his intention, I feel safer with the solid wall of muscle between me and the murderer.

"Mrs. Orange, give us the key," Dex says. The demand ignores her accusation—the misdirect at another, supposed weapon.

A branch cracks and I spy Kaley's husband creeping closer. He flanks her on the right, always the loyal puppy dog at her heels. But now he looks more like an angry wolf than a cute little pet.

"I-I don't have it," she stutters, likely from the cold.

Even accused of murder, Kaley remains confident with her nose in the air and eyes cast down at us. She gestures wildly at Dex's pants with bugged eyes. "Didn't you hear me about the gun?"

Maybe she isn't as confident as I think. Maybe it's because she's guilty of not one, but two murders.

I meet Caspian's gaze. Did Kaley kill him for choosing to marry Alex, and then she killed Alex all these years later? Did she lead us out here to trick us all? I tried to remember where she went after the clique broke apart and before Alessandra was found dead. Maybe it wasn't the spice of Jeanie's sangria I smelled, but the burning scent of Kaley's expensive perfume.

I open my mouth to ask the ghost, not even caring if everyone thinks I'm as nutty as a squirrel. It doesn't matter because I don't have time to formulate words before another voice fills the tense silence.

"You have to have the key or another weapon," Dex says, "you killed—"

In a flash, Scott dives forward, cutting Dex off with his fist. The thwack of his bony knuckles against Dex's nose sparks another round of gasps.

For the skinny vegan that Scott is, he packs a punch strong enough to send Dex stumbling back. One moment I'm staring at my ex-boyfriend's ghost, the next I'm on the ground, with my future ex-boyfriend on top of me.

9
IN THE ROSE BUSHES WITH THE GARDENING SHEARS

A shadow cast by Scott's body looms over us and the glow of half a dozen phone flashlights shine behind him. The shadowy shape of his scrawny shoulders stretches beyond us. Blood drips from somewhere, and suddenly I know how Alessandra must have felt as she fell to the ground. But I suffer no stab wound, just a woozy head and swirling stomach.

The red stains come from Dex's nose as he rolls off me. I suck in a breath of fresh air after his firm body had me pinned. If I was able to breathe in that position, I can't say I hated being so close to him. But now's not the time to think about men and how earthy and good they smell—in Dex's case. When it comes to Caspian, I'm captured by his dark chocolate eyes every time.

But it's not Caspian or Dex who's looking at me and breathing heavily, it's Scott. He shifts his raging gaze to Dex and frowns deeper. "Who are you to accuse my wife of murder?"

Kaley stares at her husband, clearly as shocked by this tough behavior as the rest of us. I follow his gaze to Dex who gets to his feet. As he straightens from crouched to standing, his T-shirt pulls up and I catch sight of something shiny. At first, I think it comes from a bedazzled belt to match his cowboy boots, but it's nothing of the sort. In fact, his belt is worn and matches the casual—if not a little wrinkled—outfit.

I squint and make out the shape of what appears to be a gun's handle. A gun? My eyebrows shoot to my hairline and spit catches in my throat. Kaley wasn't lying. My heart pounds with an erratic and violent beat.

Who *is* Dex Emerald?

Dex wipes dirt off his jeans and straightens, standing at a head taller than Scott—with the help of his heeled boots. "I'm just a concerned guy who wants to keep his neighbors safe."

Is that what the gun is for? Protection? I can only hope. Dex is hiding something, but I can't picture him hurting more than feelings. Just like he did with his blunt accusation against Kaley. He's too nonchalant and seems to joke his way through life like me. Unless that's all a cover...

Dex only sighs rather than answers the question. The moment of silence lets everyone ruminate on Scott's behavior. Did he defend her because husband and wife worked together to kill Alessandra? My mind is searching for a suspect. I want answers ASAP because answers will keep us safe.

Zyra sneaks past them to help me to my feet. Like Dex, I wipe dirt and leaves off my pants as I stand. I cringe as a twinge of pain pulses in my tailbone. Before I can subtly signal Zyra's attention to the gun, the men return to their pissing contest and pull all of our eyes to them.

"Hey!" Scott steps closer which puts his nose inches from Dex's. I almost wonder if they'll kiss—or kill—each other, right then and there. But Dex's jaw is relaxed, and he casually folds his arms across his chest, a sure signal that he doesn't want to fight. Clearly, Scott doesn't get the memo. "I asked you a question," he says through clenched teeth.

As the one aware of the weapon in Dex's pants, I feel an obligation to break the tension. Not even the suggestive idea of what's in the cowboy's jeans distracts me from my responsibility and the actual tool in his pants.

I swallow a smirk at the thought and speak up. "It's not only Dex who thinks Kaley is the killer."

Kaley snaps her neck to stare at me. Though her gaze is fiery and she looks ready to shout how wrong I am, nothing comes out of her open mouth. Her voice seems caught in her throat as she shivers, not unlike the shock I felt when I first stood close to a ghost. Except Kaley doesn't act like she can see Caspian, only feel the chill of his apparition.

"The fact is," I say, trying to sound official while I recall Kaley's behavior at the HOA meeting, "you didn't like it when Alessandra agreed to my plan."

Darla laughs a single, curt laugh that sounds more like a hiccup. "Kaley doesn't like anyone who disagrees with her."

Frank and Jeanie both mumble in agreement. Relief floods me like the feeling of finding a bathroom when I really have to go. Thorn House Road's drama crew has averted their suspicions from me to Kaley. It makes more sense, after all. Kaley is a whip-smart lawyer, and a professional twister of the truth. The only person standing in her way of being the queen of the neighborhood was the HOA president.

Scott shifts his eyes in the direction of the group but doesn't dare move his head. He holds Dex in place by blocking the narrow path with his thin frame.

My eyes focus on the woman behind them. Despite the

tight wrap of hair in the claw clip, wisps escape Kaley's bun and jut out around her head.

The question slips out before I can think it through. "Were you trying to frame me?"

Kaley opens her mouth but her husband answers first. Scott uses his wiry strength to shove past Dex's bulky arm. Like a vice, he grips my shoulders, channeling all of his cross-yoga muscles to hold me in place.

"Stop it!" he shouts. While it seemed he might lean in and plant a kiss on Dex's mouth when threatening him, Scott's energy has shifted, and I worry he'll headbutt me.

"That's my wife you're talking about," he spits and shakes me like it'll knock sense into me. But he's the one who may have lost a marble or two.

Kaley steps forward gingerly. "Scott?" Even she is cautious, wary that her husband might completely snap like a brittle branch under the sole of her shoe. Everybody is on edge. How can we not be? Scott's the only one letting it get to him and even his wife finds it worrisome based on the quiver in her voice.

"I've got this, Baby," he says.

"Are you working together?" I ask. What kind of idiot accuses the angry guy who has his hands on her? *Way to go, Olive.* But curiosity has me listening for his answer rather than recoiling from his grip.

"My wife and I always work together. We're a team," he says, words spilling out faster than he can breathe. "We do everything together because we have a great marriage..." The words don't sound real, rather a script that he's rehearsed—either to convince himself or the people around him. The forced words remind me of cheesy dialogue written into the shows on the home improvement network. His energy fades for a moment and he catches his breath.

Okay? Has he moved on from the topic of murder? Scott's rant feels personal and unrelated.

"Oh, Scott, Honey..." Kaley's voice trails off and she gingerly touches her lips. Not even in high school did I witness Kaley so emotional. I once compared her to a stone the size of a boulder, cold and never changing, never feeling and always in your way. Did the murder finally crack her, too?

Scott swings his arm to block her from stepping forward."Kales, let me defend you—"

Tears well in his wife's eyes. Are they from love or guilt?

"So you were with her when Alessandra died?" I ask.

At that, he finally blinks. His eyelashes flutter and his wild eyes shrink slightly. He glances over his shoulder at the half-dozen pairs of eyes watching him. "Well, no—but Kaley is nothing if not honest. She'd never hurt anyone, much less lie about it, or anything for that matter. So if she thinks you're the murderer, then you're the doggone murderer!"

With each word, he speaks louder and shakes me harder. His fingers dig into the flesh of my arms, and I try to pull away.

"Hey!" I hear Dex's voice in the chaos among Darla's gasps and the poodle's yips.

"Olive, is he hurting you?" Caspian's disembodied shout joins the collection of sounds. "I'll haunt him so hard..."

I tense as Scott shakes me again, maybe hoping a confession will fall out of me. Or the key. Or another weapon used to stab the HOA president who didn't approve my event center for Thorn House Road. While my brain rattles in my head, I register the chill of a ghost nearby.

Someone, probably Dex, manages to pry one of Scott's hands off of me.

"Scott, stop." Kaley sucks in a breath and she lunges forward. Her fingers wrap around her husband's wiry bicep and she pulls him off of me, once and for all.

Both Dex and Caspian insert themselves between me and my attacker, blocking Scott from grabbing me a second time. When my mind settles, heat rises in my cheeks. Why am I blushing over the fact that two men rescued me when one is clearly a spy and the other's a ghost?

Okay, so Dex might not be a spy, but he carries a concealed weapon and fancies himself a detective of some sort. Still, they're protecting me and I'm flattered. It's easier to focus on this piece of positivity than think of Scott's little attack, and what he and his guilty wife might do next.

Zyra links her arm through mine and pulls me two steps back. This gently puts distance between me and the fight, though the chaos has fizzled.

Scott stares, open-mouthed, at his teary-eyed wife—a woman I've never witnessed as dishelved as she is now.

"I'm not honest," she says, still shivering, though Caspian no longer touches her. Her shoulders shake more violently than before as a sob builds.

Darla hums in agreement but nobody pays her any attention.

"No, you are." Scott says, taking her into his arms. "You're my perfect queen—"

"Oh, screw this!" She yanks away from his hug. "I've told you not to call me that. Especially not in public and—"

A gasp cuts her off and her eyes go wide, just as they did when she pointed at Dex's gun. This time, she stares right through Caspian. Or maybe at him.

We all freeze, hinging on her next action. Will she snap

and try to stab us all? Or will she allow her husband to snap on her behalf, for his queen? Maybe she'll scream *ghost* and everyone will scramble like sheep at the sound of a wolf's howl.

We wait. Not blinking or breathing in case we miss a moment.

Nothing exciting happens at all. In fact, it's the most boring reaction I've ever witnessed from Kaley. Her shoulders slump, and when she folds her arms, it seems she's resigned to accept whatever shocked her.

"Come on, Scott," she says. "Just admit you know I tried to cheat."

"Of course I knew, but didn't you just say we're in public?" he says through gritted teeth. His eyes shift to the group, then back to his wife. "Do you want people to hear about this?"

"Ha!" Kaley laughs. "Who cares anymore?" She steps back, throwing her arms wide, which reaches across the width of the narrow passage. Leaves shuffle as her fingers brush against them. "I'm tired of hiding. Alessandra is dead. We're trapped in here with a murderer and everyone is accusing me." She stabs at her chest with a sharp fingernail. "Me! Can you believe it? The only person trying to defend the property values and aesthetic of Thorn House Road. If you want to know my secret, there it is. My marriage is a facade. I lie about loving my husband, but I'm telling the whole truth and nothing but the truth about my loyalty to my friend Alessandra. I. Did not kill. Anyone."

We believe her. I know we all do based on the sudden shifting eyes—the gazes that creep from one person to another. Suspicion has moved on from the woman we thought we'd identified as the most dangerous of the group.

I meet my daughter's eyes and raise my brows. *Are you thinking what I'm thinking?*

If Kaley didn't want Alessandra out of her way, then who killed the HOA president? And will they kill again?

My gaze falls to the lump under Dex's shirt. Is that gun for protection? Or did Dex defend me only because I trust him...for now? Will he turn on us later?

Caspian's voice comes out breathy and faint. "A facade..." he says. He turns, flickering between a solid manifestation and the glowing wisp of a ghost. "My marriage was going to be a facade, too. Maybe Kaley was right when she told me Alex was using me because I remember trying to have a private talk with Alex before we walked down the aisle. I found her in her dressing room at Thorn House. We were getting married here. I asked her why she wanted to marry me and she refused to answer." His voice grows stronger, from a fading breath to a confident tone. "I don't think Alex ever loved me."

Another memory. Another clue.

I swallow and nod, signaling that I heard him. His epiphany is important, but not as imperative as the weapon in the pants of a potential killer. Maybe Caspian's snide remarks about Dex never came from jealousy, and my dead ex-boyfriend was right all along. Maybe Dex has more than a gun to hide.

10
BY THE GHOST WITH THE GUN

Though Zyra is likely stronger, faster, and more observant than me, I'm still her mother. I link my arm through hers and tug her close as a form of protection. I can't trust anyone in this maze except for her, and she needs to know I'll do anything to keep her safe.

I want to take a sidebar and chat with Caspian about his revelation. For now, I'm busy keeping our daughter safe. She huddles against me as we shuffle along, not cold or scared, but connected and ready to take on the world.

By returning to follow in Kaley's footsteps, the group has silently accepted she isn't a killer. She's smart, and a leader, and until Caspian corrects her direction, I let her guide us through the maze I can't remember.

I zone out, eyes glazed as I stare at the back of her blonde head between Darla and Oscar. Dex walks two paces behind them and Jeanie is up front again, dragging Frank along to keep up with Kaley. Scott falls behind, dejected, with his bony shoulders slumped and his suit coat nearly sliding off his arms. The guy's dirty laundry—or rather, his sad love life—was just announced in front of the entire neighborhood.

"You keep staring at nothing," Zyra whispers. "Reminds me of *the look* from your show."

She refers to a momentary pause—one of my signature behaviors from the home improvement channel's show. I was known for walking into a home or a room and going completely still, like a statue, with my gaze at the space for approximately two seconds and then at the camera for another eight seconds. My co-hosts called it the *psychic freeze* like a medium or seer in a paranormal TV show who stops to absorb a sudden vision. I shake the memory away before it conjures all the feelings. If I think about the network and my old show for too long, I might miss it and give up on my the new adventure I've come to enjoy.

"I see dead people," I say.

She laughs and shakes her head, having no idea it's the truth. It's not an inappropriate joke in the wake of the HOA president's death. It's a fact.

Seemingly inappropriate or not, Zyra doesn't chide me for it. This is how we've always survived: together, on coffee and jokes, and with a dream. Arms linked, we stand against the world, thriving with our passions—her obsession with college and my addiction to decoration. I swallow a lump in my throat and imagine the squeezing feeling comes from my career at the channel. I shove it down for now. I like being an event hostess, but will I lose this job, too?

I tilt my head to bump hers gently. "Are you okay?"

"Never better," she whispers, flashing me a quick, beaming grin.

I twist my expression into disbelief. "You do know we're trapped in a giant maze with a murderer, right?"

She smirks and becomes the perfect image of Caspian's

expression when he makes a cheeky comment. "Do you have any idea how impactful this life experience will look on my college essay?" She exhales through her nose.

I nod, lips curled down as I consider this. "Impressive positive spin on the situation. I take back the detective suggestion. You should become a mindset guru."

Zyra's hair brushes against my cheek as she shakes her head. "Neither. I'm still gunning for forensic science."

Speaking of guns... I glance at Caspian who has melted into the bushes. With the passageway only wide enough to fit two people side-by-side, he walks inside the plants as he keeps pace with me.

He must sense me looking because he snaps his attention from Dex to me. I nod, guessing that his clenched jaw and creased forehead means he's worried about the weapon too.

"I know you can't talk back right now," he says. "You'll sound crazy."

I acknowledge it with a slight smile.

"I'm trying to recall why I ever asked Alex to marry me," he says, giving me a side-glance then dropping his gaze to his feet that never quite touch the ground. Maybe his worry lines have nothing to do with the gun. In fact, Caspian doesn't keep his eye on Dex anymore. Doesn't he see the weapon in the guy's pants? "I don't remember loving anyone else—" he stops, clamping his jaw shut for a moment and then releasing a breath.

I narrow my eyes, signaling curiosity. *Tell me more.* I use the same look I gave him years ago when he told me he loved me for the first time. It was two weeks before prom when he asked me to be his date with a paper rose. He made it out of red paint swatches from the home improvement store. Like Zyra, even as a teenager, I knew exactly what I wanted to be when I grew up and I shared that with Caspian daily. Of course now, I'm waffling between careers and can no longer claim that level of confidence.

After I said yes to his private promposal and planted a giant kiss on his mouth, he was breathless and let the word *love* slip between gasps. With one look at my expression, my narrowed eyes encouraged him to keep talking. *Oliveyou.* So, his first time was a jumbled mess of my name and *I love you* but it made us both burst out laughing in the middle of the quiet school hallway after we ditched class together.

Now, he chews on his lip, but it doesn't suppress the smirk—the same smirk his daughter gave me only minutes ago. Caspian knows I'm prodding him to reveal more.

"Anyway," he says with a sigh as he stretches one arm and rakes his fingers through his hair. The more his memory fills in, the shyer he seems to become. At the first ghost sighting, he threw around our old jokes and innuendos. But now, Caspian keeps to the topic of conversation and I sense his embarrassment. Does he regret going no-contact with us as much as I regret running away?

"I think I did it for my parents," he says. "I remember my father introducing me to Alex. She was the daughter of someone he knew from his golf club. Our relationship was fast, too." He shakes his head. "We were only dating for a few weeks when my father said I should buy her a ring. He said she was good for me."

My memory is fuzzy when it comes to Caspian's parents. I recall their rough edges and how they made me feel, along with the rest of the snobs on Thorn House Road when my pregnancy came out. I can't remember them ever speaking to me directly. As the daughter of a single father, a carpenter, and not a man who could afford membership at a golf club, I suppose they didn't see me as worthy of a ring. I wasn't from an affluent, old-money family, after all.

Leaves crunch underfoot, the only sound among ten people. Not even Darla breaks the silence with a snide remark to spark a bit of gossip. I wonder if we're collectively ashamed for accusing Kaley. In our desperation, we pushed her to confess her deepest secret that embarrassed both her and Scott. I know I feel a little guilt. The tears that welled in his eyes after Kaley's announcement only solidified my pity for her husband.

I have no ill will toward him, though I don't love how easily he was provoked into a fight, or that his temper left me shaken. Maybe he thought punching Dex in his wife's honor was a brave thing to do. To a group already on edge, it only made us jumpier rather than impressed.

The poodle yawns, his wet, black snout poking out from behind Oscar's thick arm. I scan each person in front of us. Jeanie doesn't have a weapon. Frank was never a suspect since he was in the restroom at the time of the murder. My gaze falls on Darla, who is low on my list of suspects. She's too talkative to keep a secret and doesn't have a motive. Besides, she's too short to have stabbed Alessandra, the model-esque woman in heels. At least without some serious effort that I suspect would be impossible with her arthritic shoulders. And what about the man next to her? Oscar claims to have killed people in some unknown war, but does that make him dangerous here and now? He's certainly big enough to overpower Alessandra and maybe practiced in taking someone out...discreetly.

Or there's Dex.

A little sigh escapes me. I like talking with him. I like his presence, and his smirks remind me of Caspian. But liking someone doesn't make them innocent.

As if reading my mind, Dex's attention turns to us. The thick swoop of sandy hair falls into his face and the smile lines around his mouth hint at a lifetime of joking and good humor. He glances over his shoulder and slows his pace, twisting to face us halfway as we walk.

"Are we on the same page?" Dex asks as he shoves his hands into his worn-out jeans. At least in his pockets, he can't easily reach for his gun. His eyes flicks to the man bringing up the rear, then back to us, and then to Scott once more. I assume his shifting gaze is a nod toward the person Dex wants us to consider a suspect.

Zyra tilts her head side-to-side, considering this before quietly adding her two cents. "Maybe. Or maybe Scott was just defending his wife."

"Jeanie had an outburst too," I say, "and we were wrong about her." Are his speculations meant to keep us from considering him? I glare at him and feel Caspian's chill on my left shoulder. He's close, maybe ready to insert himself between us if Dex gets dangerous. But what can a ghost do other than give Dex the chills and make him wish he had his flannel?

"Why are you staring at him like that?" Caspian asks.

I glimpse the ghost at my side, shooting him a knowing glare that I direct back to Dex. I mouth the words *you were right.*

To my complete shock, Caspian sighs. "I think I let my jealousy get to me. Dex seems like a good guy."

My eyes bug and I shift them back and forth, signaling for him to check out the weapon tucked into Dex's jeans. How does my ex-boyfriend go from accusing the guy to ignoring the proof that he's dangerous?

We walk with purpose now, picking up the pace as the breeze dips colder. The night is in full swing with a half-moon overhead. The weak glow casts odd shapes through the sparser sections of the hedges.

Zyra sighs and finally nods in agreement with my statement. "Everybody is on edge. I'm more keen to worry about the calm ones."

Like you. I glare at Dex despite Caspian's off-the-wall comment. Did I let Dex's relaxed approach lull me into a false sense of security? What is his game? What brought a farmer to Thorn House Road?

"We agree it's not Kaley, Jeanie, or Frank, right?" Dex counts off the names on his fingers, a charming characteristic that I try to ignore. Our pace instinctively slows even more as we put distance between us and those ahead. We don't want them to overhear our suspicions. "That leaves Darla, Scott, and Oscar. If we go with the calm-person hypothesis, then I say we keep a close eye on Oscar. He's quiet and I'm curious why he helps Darla so often. Is it to make him appear kind and innocent?"

Zyra leans away from me to look past Dex. It seems she's scanning Oscar. Once she agrees, she purses her lips and nods. "But what's his motive?"

The better question is, what's Dex's motive?

"Why did you move to Thorn House Road?" I blurt.

Dex's eyebrows flick. "What? Because I hit it big—"

"Right, right, striking gold in the corn industry. You're supposedly a big farmer man," I say, irritation bubbling. The guy's buddy-buddy behavior is no longer going to trick me. Why carry a gun to a garden party?

Zyra nudges me, and I suspect it's to discourage me from word vomiting. I don't mean to be rude, but if rude is the only way to get answers, then so be it.

"Yeah," he says with an unconvincing shrug. "I moved in the same day as you."

"Sure. So when did you have time to get so chummy with Alessandra? You know, to find out that Jeanie has a boring secret?"

He cocks his head and opens his mouth but remains speechless. The wind rushes through the thick walls of green and tosses his hair around. His face remains still, brows furrowed as he makes sense of what I've said.

Zyra slips her arm from mine. I feel her and Caspian's gaze on me. I avoid glancing at them, and keep them in the corner of my eye instead. If I look and see their matching expressions, like father like daughter, I might cry. Getting irritated often leads to tears of frustration for me, and I was already plenty annoyed with Dex for pretending to be my friend.

"Well, I go to the HOA meetings," he explains. "I stayed after the last one to chat with Alessandra about gardening rules."

"So you were alone with Alessandra only days before she was killed?"

He stops walking, and I nearly collide into him. I freeze and manage to save my nose from smacking into his chin.

Scott squeezes past us, without so much as lifting his head out of curiosity. My gaze tracks him for a moment as he saunters along, following behind Oscar and Darla. The poor guy looks like Charlie Brown after Lucy tricked him into trying to kick the football.

I swallow and look at Dex who is inches from my face and still staring at me. He's frozen. *Good. Let him sweat.* Though his crossed arms and pursed lips don't indicate concern, and instead of body odor or sweat, he smells like saltwater and soil and mint. The combination briefly sweeps my imagination to a beachy forest.

Dem you and your intoxicating scent.

I blink and focus on the next question. Caspian's body chills me as he stands closer. Has the jealousy returned, or is he seeing my point of view? Either way, he's on my side.

"Why the interrogation?" Caspian asks.

"What's with the third degree?" Dex says at the same time as Caspian and their voices overlap. Other than Dex's faint southern accent, they sound similar.

"Mom?" Zyra pipes up, curious about my train of thought.

Just hearing her makes me want answer faster. Too many voices have distracted me from getting to the bottom of what's concealed by Dex's bottom. I need to speed this interrogation along.

"Where were you when Alessandra was killed?" I lift my hand and poke him right in the center of his chest. "You said you saw me and knew I was on the other side of the yard. But why were you watching me? Did you want to make sure I didn't see you attack her?"

"What?" Genuine shock drops his jaw. "I'm not the killer!" Though the volume of his voice jumped, it isn't loud enough to pique anyone's interest. The group disappears around the corner at the end of another bushy passageway.

Demmit. Now I've really gone and screwed the pooch by separating us from the group. We're alone with the guy carrying a weapon—but not for long, if I can get it away from him. It's now or never, and thankfully, I'm close enough to reach for the gun.

11
LEFT BEHIND WITH THE LIAR

Before Dex can react, I snake my arm around his waist and find the cold hilt of the gun. I wrap my fingers around it and yank it from his pants. Either I have dormant action hero reflexes, or I simply catch Dex off guard. He doesn't move to stop me and I succeed in stealing the weapon.

"Then why do you have this?" I hold it up, my hand shaking with a gun in its grip.

His eyes nearly cross as he peers down at the barrel under his nose. I don't hold it up to threaten him, but to make a point.

"Check it," he says casually. "It's not loaded."

I relax slightly, bringing the gun lower as I examine it. It's lightweight which seems to corroborate his statement. But when he unfolds his arms and reaches for something in his front pocket, I flip the gun around, gripping it as though I know how to use it.

"Zyra, save yourself," I say, though I know his jeans are far too tight in the front to conceal anything too dangerous. And I still have his pocketknife in my pants. Plus,

Alessandra was stabbed, not shot. My knuckles turn white with the intense grip I have on the gun because these pieces of information don't make me any more comfortable with Dex's secrets.

His chuckle infuriates me. He holds up one palm in surrender and digs into his pocket with his other hand. "I'm getting my badge."

"Your...what?" My brain doesn't register the explanation.

He pulls out a small black wallet and flips it open. When he holds it to my face, I'm forced to acknowledge the shiny golden badge and an identification card with his picture on it.

Central Intelligence Agency. Special Agent Declan Green.

"No freaking way," I say. "This can't be real. It's not even the right name!"

"Dex Emerald is my alias," he says as he shifts to show Zyra the identification and badge. She momentarily squints, whispering as she reads the words in the fine lettering. Caspian drifts to her side and inspects the CIA identification with the same scrunched expression.

"It has the right engraving and a serial number," she says.

With that, Dex flicks the black holder shut, tucks it into his pocket, and then plucks the gun from my hand with two fingers.

I want to punch him for lying, but he's already bruised from where Scott's fist connected with his face.

"You're really CIA?"

He smirks. "My mom doesn't believe it either, and she's visited me at work. I was a bit of a screwup in my formative years."

No wonder we hit it off so easily. If that's true, he's

defied the odds of nearly ruining his life at a young age—just like me. Though I can't claim success at the home improvement network anymore. I shove the thought away.

"Okay, neat." I try to wrap my head around this new piece of information. "I knew you weren't a farmer. Farmers don't move to snobby suburbs and abide by HOA rules. Now, explain what a CIA agent is doing at a boring place like Thorn House Road?"

Dex chuckles again. "Sounds like a pickup line."

"Huh," Caspian says with a snort. "I was thinking the same thing. I kind of like this guy."

I shoot him a quick and frustrated glare. Only an hour ago, he basically called Dex a murderer.

"What?" His ghostly shoulders shrug and he smiles sadly—a look an ex-boyfriend might give once he's accepted that his former lover has moved on. "He stood up for you when Kaley got temperamental. I didn't even do that for you when I was a real person. And now..." his gaze drops to his feet where they float just inches above the weeds. "I can't help you or our daughter at all."

"I'm undercover," Dex says, pulling me from Caspian's existential crisis.

It explains Caspian's jealous confession and the shift in attitude toward Dex. He's not wrong. Dex has been nothing but helpful since we got trapped. Maybe the gun really is for protection.

The stress of the garden party stacked onto the ghost's haunting and now a murder investigation has done a number on my logical thinking. Even I, Queen of Rambling and Talking Too Fast, can't keep up with this break-neck pace of predictions and unveiled truths. I want answers but maybe accusing everyone of murder isn't the way to find the killer and keep my daughter safe.

I force myself to slow down and take a deep breath. With a few rapid blinks, I focus on Dex's handsome face again. *Thank heavens the guy I have a little crush on isn't the killer.* I've made bad decisions before, but nothing of that magnitude.

Dex meets my gaze. "I'm tracking someone who might be building a weapon."

"Building a weapon?" All I can do is echo him. Taking a breath didn't help, because my brain still takes too long to catch up. All the distractions, from ghostly entities, to murderous neighbors and my daughter's safety, don't help. My attention is split in a dozen different directions, and I need to focus like a detective.

He nods and returns the gun to its safe spot under his shirt, this time tucking it in the front of his jeans between his hip and belly button with the barrel down. "We believe it is a team of people. We found their previous hideout earlier this month, but they moved the chemicals quickly. Someone here has purchased copious amounts of illegal fertilizer, and we've yet to track where it went."

"Fertilizer?" Zyra asks. "Like a bomb?" She pieces it together, as a little gasp tightens her voice. "That's so scary!"

We fall silent for a moment. Dex's behavior makes sense now: the way he observes silently, acts like a detective, and the double personalities. It seems he's a light-hearted guy and those natural tendencies often slip through his serious persona while on the job.

The wind makes the leaves clap. Goosebumps prickle on my bare arms. *Fertilizer? Crap.* My mind conjures images of the grass I brought back from the dead—all in the hopes of gaining the HOA president's approval.

The calming white noise of the wind clears my head

enough to realize I'm the person Dex is tracking. My heart pounds wildly, and just when I've wrangled control of my mouth, I lose track of my nerves. Apparently, ridiculously cheap products sold by sketchy guys on Facebook are not the steal I think they are. My thumping pulse ramps until I can't take it anymore.

I slap my palms to my cheeks. "It's me," I confess.

All three of them cock their heads at me, clueless, until Zyra gasps.

"Oh, my gosh it *is* you!" she says, her jaw dropping.

Dex's gaze ping-pongs between us. "So you're saying you're the killer?"

I scrunch my face. "Kill her who?" His question takes a moment for my brain to understand. He thinks my confession is about the murder. "No, no, I meant I'm the bomb builder—"

"Mom!" Zyra squeals.

"Smooth," Caspian says.

I shake my head. My tongue moves too fast and I've lost control of it again. "I mean, I bought the fertilizer."

Dex's brows shoot to where his hair hangs over his forehead. The look is swoony, and I'm convinced he's a real life Fox Mulder now that I know he's a special agent.

"For..." his voice trails off.

"For fertilizer," I squeak, pointing at the ground as if that explains everything. Perhaps too eagerly, I rip off a leaf from the hedges and wave it around. It wiggles back and forth limply. "You know? To make grass grow. If I got cell service out here, I'd show you the Facebook profile of the guy I bought it from."

"Was this guy from Fernbridge County?" he asks. I nod and he pinches the bridge of his nose. "Ah, it's starting to make sense. He pawned his lot off on you, which means I'm on the wrong track. Ugh." A muttered curse slips from him as he places his hands on his hips. The position stretches his tight shirt across his chest.

"Sorry?" I say with a weak shrug.

Dex waves the apology away like a bug buzzing in his face. "It's not your fault. I'm off my game lately. I might be taking a step down to a local police force after this."

"That's gotta hurt," Caspian says, sucking air through his teeth. Apparently, his ghostly frame is strong enough to move air, but nothing else.

I ignore him and march past both guys, heading for the end of the passage. It's time we catch up with the group before another body drops. Now that I know Dex is the safe space I was hoping for, that means the killer is up ahead. This is still my garden party and I'm determined not to let another person get hurt.

We resume the hike through the hedges, listening for the echo of Darla's distant yammering. Through the wind and rustle of leaves, it's impossible to make out her words but I recognize the conspiratorial tone of voice, after having known Darla since I was a kid. She's gossiping.

"So, as an agent," I start, feeling suddenly shy and giggly around Dex. The feeling dissipates when he raises his eyebrows to indicate he's listening. I might have a crush and a few nerves rattling around because of it, but Dex's personality is warm and comfortable. "Who do you think we should be watching out for?"

"You," he smirks and cranes his neck to look at me as we walk. "Did you know the fertilizer was illegal?"

"Of course not," I say as I duck under a long, wobbly branch that reaches halfway across the passageway.

With a gentle touch, he rubs at his nose where Scott's fist landed. "I want to say the guy with the most to hide is the one who hit me. He's the person most capable of violence in my mind. But that's only a guess, and obviously, I've been off my game."

I nod and squint at the dark lines blooming under his eyes. In a couple of hours, he'll likely look like a raccoon with two black circles around his baby blues. Even then, I suspect he'll be just as attractive.

He smirks. "I might still have to arrest you when we get out of here."

My head snaps in his direction. "Seriously?"

"No." He laughs and brushes the swoop of hair from his face. My teen crush senses are tingling but it isn't because he looks like my favorite *X-Files* star. Dex and I feel like old friends. "But I do need something to show for the time I've spent here."

I stick my nose in the air, feigning arrogance with a hint of a smile. Dex is easy to joke with and talk to. Relief floods me now that I know he's innocent, and the warm feeling of romantic interest returns. "Hmm, well, you'll have to catch me first."

"She's a terrible runner," Caspian says as if Dex can hear him. His ghostly figure inserts itself between us for a moment, sending chills down my arm.

When no one else is looking, I point two fingers at my eyes and then direct them to Caspian.

"What?" he asks nonchalantly, but I notice him looking at the goosebumps on my arms. He slowly drifts back, allowing me to space apart from his cold existence and to feel the warmth of Dex walking beside me again. "You should tell Dex that so he'll be ready to have your back in case the killer comes for you. Besides, it wouldn't hurt to get to know him. He seems...like your type."

My eyebrows flicker. Is my ex-boyfriend trying to set me

up? Or does he sense my little crush on Dex and this is his way of encouraging me to move on? Of course, I moved on years ago, but seeing him again brought back a few emotions I didn't expect. Does he know I wish I could hug him? One last time?

"Don't overthink it," Caspian says, anticipating my questions. "I'm only saying you seem to get along with him. You don't have to marry the guy."

I hum in agreement and drop my voice to a minuscule whisper. "I'm a husband-free kind of gal. No weddings for me unless I'm hosting them."

Caspian freezes and I stop with him while Zyra and Dex continue around on into the stretching abyss of hedge hallways.

"Husband..." he breathes, eyes glazing over. Recognition dawns in his dark gaze. "My memory is coming back in pieces. It was at my wedding that someone came after me with the key. A man, somebody's husband—" he snaps his fingers but it makes no noise. His eyes search the ground until his gaze lands on me again. "It was Scott. He was so mad when he found out Kaley wanted me to ditch the wedding and be with her. He had the key in his hand and... and...crap!" He takes a swing of his open palm at the hedges but it only slightly rustles the leaves. "I can't remember what he said."

Scott. The same guy who attacked Dex, and acted like a dejected Charlie Brown. The mood swings definitely point to unstable behavior. But what motive does he have to kill Alessandra, his wife's friend and the woman who was supposed to marry the guy he hated?

Still, it makes more sense than Darla or Oscar attacking the HOA president. Both of them have lived here long enough to overrule Alessandra's ideas, and I've yet to hear

Darla gossip about her. And if Scott tried to attack with the key back then, it's possible that's the weapon he used on Alessandra, too.

Did Scott carry revenge for Caspian all these years and take it out on the woman Caspian left at the altar? Did he stab her in the heart after Kaley broke his?

The night fell silent. No wind. No poodle barks or Darla's echoing gossip. Not even the crunch of leaves underfoot can be heard.

Caspian's gaze met mine. At the same time, we turn and bolt after Zyra, hoping she didn't catch up to the group... and Scott.

12
GROUP CHAT WITH THE GOSSIP

Since Caspian can do spooky things like walk through walls of branches and thick leaves, he finds our daughter first. The jog there reminds me that my ex is right, I'm a terrible runner. Huffing and puffing, I nearly collapse as I reach Zyra and Dex.

Upon hearing my dramatic wheezing, my daughter spins around.

"Are you okay?" she asks. "You look like you've seen a—"

I hold up my hand to stop her before she says the word out loud. It saddens me to think of her saying *ghost* in front of the father she'll never meet. He stands right beside her, but she can't see him, and that's enough to make anyone a little teary-eyed.

"Just...wanted to catch up," I say between breaths. A cramp twinges at my side and I lean over, hands on my thighs. Thankfully, Dex does seem to have my back. If Scott decides to go on a stabbing spree, I won't be able to outrun him—especially not with all that cross-yoga he does.

Now that I can breathe, I notice our surroundings.

We've come to the longest, narrowest passageway yet. As an interior designer, I'm often good with approximating measurements, but this seems to span on and on. Is it across an acre? Two miles? A thousand? Maybe it's the time of night that strikes me as endless. This stretch is darker because the hedges are taller and the most overgrown. I guess we're almost at the center of the maze.

In the previous twists and turns, the branches reach across the walking space, but some were already trampled and smashed from trespassers. Here, this deep inside the labyrinth, the teenagers don't dare venture. Or so it appears. Maybe Jeanie's daughter and her boyfriend made it out this far but were careful not to leave tracks.

Jeanie is out of my line of sight now. I can't see anybody past Oscar, whose thick shoulders fill the entire passageway. Because of the long branches that sway high above, he has to duck every so often or risk getting scratches across his bald skull. Only me, Zyra, Dex, and the killer bring up the caboose. Perhaps Oscar knows about Scott, and that's why he's keeping Darla in front of him and out of stabbing range. Their attached-at-the-hip behavior is a new addition. As far as I remember from years ago, Darla Prune and Oscar Sparrow were never friends. In fact, they used to argue over property lines since they shared a fence. Now they're sticking by one another's sides more than the husbands and wives of the group.

The poodle growls as the wind picks up again. The pup's faint, low grumbling turns to whimpers. I suspect Darla pets her furbaby because Oscar's pace has slowed and the growling stops.

"My Gassy doesn't seem to like you, Frank," Darla says, unashamed as usual. She has no trouble speaking her mind or pointing blame.

Frank only laughs.

Undaunted, Darla continues. "It must be nice not to be the new family in the neighborhood anymore." She says it in a tone that suggests she's hoping to stir a conversation.

In this dark passageway, we've fallen silent. Only the sounds of hiking and breathing fill the night. With all the walking, talking, and sleuthing, we're tired. Everybody drags their feet and slouches, feeling as though the maze will never end. We'll never get out of here, and the killer will never be served justice.

Nobody responds to Darla's comment, so she keeps going. "Well, I know there isn't a perfect person among us, but I'd like to believe Alessandra's death was an accident."

"A lady doesn't get stabbed in the heart by accident, Darla," Kaley shouts from the front of the line.

Though Kaley is technically my nemesis, I have to agree with her. That wound was no accident. A gaping hole in the center of one's chest doesn't come from a trip and a fall.

"Fine then," Darla says, "if there is a murderer among us, then I think we should make the killer walk in front. That way they can't hurt anyone else."

"Genius!" Kaley yells again, exasperated. I hear a slap and guess it's likely her hand against her thigh or a clap to mock the elderly woman's suggestion.

"Wouldn't we have to know who the killer is in order to do that?" Frank asks in his southern drawl. His pronunciations have returned to normal since he's slowly nursing what little of his beer he has left rather than gulping down the alcohol.

Caspian and I exchange a glance, but Dex seems to think I'm looking at him. They're both flanking me on the left while Zyra walks just ahead of me on the right. None of us can squeeze side-by-side at this section of the passageway.

Dex gives me a slight nod after shifting his gaze to Scott and then back at me. Is he thinking what I'm thinking? It might be the time to share what our sleuthing skills have uncovered about Scott.

"Scott?" Dex mouths the words and then gently taps the red mark on his nose.

My ex points to Dex as if agreeing with him. Caspian purses his lips and tilts his head. "This guy knows what's up. He seems like a good detective when he's not tracking fertilizer." He snorts at the little dig, but it's obvious Dex has grown on Caspian in the past couple of hours. I suppose seeing another guy protect two women that you care for can do that. Maybe Caspian never stopped caring for me; maybe he was just a coward who never went after what he wanted against his father's wishes.

Both guys share a similar, knowing expression. Despite what Kaley's rude response might make one believe, Darla's idea isn't so outlandish. If we can make a good guess at the killer, we'll stay safer with their back turned to us. Maybe Oscar will even agree to be the bouncer and use his body to block the suspect from us.

The best part is, Dex and I have a good guess—really good, thanks to Caspian's insight. All we have to do is find the murder weapon in Scott's possession.

I shuffle, slowing my pace and then drop my voice. "Can we pickpocket the key from Scott?"

Dex shrugs. "Why do it discreetly? We want others to see if he's the one carrying it."

"True." I squint at Scott's back where his suit jacket is wrinkled over his wiry shoulders and the collar is twisted and tucked under. I'm surprised Kaley didn't force him to change. Of course, they have different styles—Scott with his online influencer vibes, and Kaley as the professional lawyer. Maybe she doesn't care enough about the guy she doesn't love to fix his collar or straighten his tie. And as the vegan fitness guru, I doubt he knows how to dress himself outside of tight yoga shorts and tank tops with his YouTube channel across the front.

"You know," I speak up, loud enough to stretch the sound to Kaley. "I think Darla's onto something."

"You do?" Darla's voice is filled with curious delight.

"It's a waste of time to speculate," Kaley shouts back. "Just like when you accused me." Is she covering for her husband? It doesn't seem so, considering her friendship with Alessandra is more genuine than her marriage to Scott.

I glance at Dex and Caspian. Dex nods eagerly while Caspian shoots me a thumbs up, encouraging me to continue. They're two sides of the same dorky coin, and I can't help but smirk.

"Look, I've got my daughter here to watch out for," I say, trying to raise my voice to reach over Oscar's shoulders again. "I want her in the safest possible place while we find our way out."

It's the whole truth and nothing but the truth. I know Zyra enjoys the investigation, the unknown, and the possibility of this story on her college essay someday, but she's likely a little frightened, too. We *all* should be. After all, we're lost in the middle of a maze, in the darkness, at the dead of night.

A shiver trickles through me.

"So I vote Scott walks up front," I say, confidently.

"Excuse me?" Scott stops and whirls around. Curiosity has everyone else doing the same. Heads bob and necks crane to get a look at the end of the line where Scott and I face off in a staring contest.

As if my accusation is Moses, bodies part like the Red Sea, and I spy Kaley's expression at the other end of the line. She's frustrated but doesn't look offended, and it bolsters my confidence in my choice. Even Scott's wife won't jump to defend him, and maybe it's because she knows he's capable of murder.

Scott laughs and folds his arms. His bony shoulders pull up the sleeves of his ill-fitted suit. "Are we really going to go through this again? What motive would I have?"

"You hated Caspian," I say before I can stop myself. It's true, anyway. And those who've been around Thorn House Road long enough likely only need this refresher to remember. A twinge of guilt stirs in my stomach and I glance at Kaley. We're not exactly friends, but I don't like that I have to embarrass her again to get to the truth. I swallow the guilt and resign to apologize or offer her comfort later. "You knew your wife was going to leave you for him, so you went after Caspian with the key on his wedding day. Maybe Alessandra was a witness to that."

Dex clears his throat. This is news to him, and I hope he doesn't think I'm keeping secrets. The clues are getting mixed up in my head. What information have I learned from my ex-boyfriend's ghost and which clues did we uncover together?

Scott only scoffs, but his darting eyes denote fear.

"But Scott was never at the wedding," Oscar says. "I remember Darla talking about how Mrs. Orange was sitting alone on the bride's side right in the middle of the front yard."

"Oh Scott was there," Kaley says. Branches crunch under Kaley's marching steps. She forces her way through the group, picking through leaves. "He just never came and sat next to me, but I thought that meant he'd left..." A branch snags her bun and pulls a chunk of hair free from the once pristine style. She squeezes past Darla and Oscar, narrowly avoiding a lick from the poodle.

Once she's within reach, she shoves her husband. "Did you kill my best friend?" Fury flickers in her eyes, and the escaped wisps of hair that frame her face match the image of a woman tired and burnt out. "I can't believe I'm agreeing with Olive, but I remember that. Caspian told me you threatened to lock him in the maze if you didn't come clean to Alessandra the day before the wedding. Did you threaten him again the next day? You wanted him to hurt as much as I hurt you, didn't you?"

Scott scoffs, but his look of indignation quickly falls. "So what if I wanted that jerk to suffer?"

"I'm confused," Oscar chimes in again. "Caspian died from a fall. I was there. Miss Alessandra and Mr. Blanc hired me to be the wedding officiant. The way he died is not well known. His parents didn't want rumors spreading about what happened in case it was ruled a suicide. What's any this have to do with Miss Alessandra getting stabbed?"

Died from a fall? Does that mean Caspian's memories are wrong? His dark eyes meet mine and we share a moment of confusion and worry. Maybe we can't rely on the moments he's recalling. Or maybe Scott's threat has nothing to do with Caspian's death. Fall injuries look wildly different from a stab to the heart with an iron key.

"I think he's right," Caspian says, brows furrowed. "I wish that day was clearer. I remember hands coming at me right before I died, but they weren't holding anything, that must have been earlier. And then... I don't know."

Empty hands means Caspian wasn't stabbed with the

key or anything else. Was he pushed? I eye Oscar, a man strong enough to knock Caspian off his feet. It might explain the blood on the side of Caspian's head. But why would Oscar draw attention to himself now if he's guilty? Or was this reverse psychology? Does he want us to know he was the officiant because he thinks that clears our suspicions?

"We were all there," Darla says. "It doesn't mean we know what happened."

I find myself watching Zyra. How does it feel to hear these strangers talking about her father's death? My chest tightens and I step up to link my arm through hers. She faintly acknowledges me with a glance and moves her arm to let me fully wrap mine through hers.

"Not all of us," Frank says. "I don't even know who this Caspian is."

Kaley's eyes brim with tears. "Alessandra deserved better."

"I know!" Scott says, opening his arms to his wife. He takes her hands, but she pulls away, nearly bumping into Oscar behind her. This time, the poodle succeeds in sneaking a lick on Kaley's cheek. "That's why I told Caspian to confess the truth about you two to Alessandra. She deserved to know before she married him."

"Nothing happened between me and Caspian, you fool," Kaley says in a low growl as if she's switched places with the dog. The poodle beside her head plays the role of the refined creature with his two front paws crossed over Oscar's wrist, while Kaley's the one who snarls. "You threatened him for nothing. Don't tell me you killed him."

"I didn't," Scott says. He raises his hands in surrender. "I swear on the essence of cross-yoga, I did not."

At that, Kaley's shoulders dip, and it seems she's

accepted his answer. Perhaps swearing on cross-yoga is Scott's tell. The look on his hollow face certainly denotes confidence. Either he's the best liar on the planet, or he's telling the truth—Scott Orange didn't kill Caspian. Then who killed Caspian on his wedding day? And did it have anything to do with his fiancée's death on the same property, all these years later?

Dex lightly touches my shoulder. His hand is warm as he gently squeezes past me. "I have an idea," he says, loud enough to announce it to the entire group. "I should have thought of this hours ago, but I'm...off my game." He mumbles the latter part of the sentence and I suspect only Zyra and I caught it. "Everybody empty their pockets and purses. Let's prove our innocence and show we don't have the key or any sharp object marked with blood."

The group is silent. Why didn't we think of that before? We were so sure we could pin the murder on Jeanie, and then Kaley, and now Scott. But in light of Caspian's manner of death, I'm not convinced anymore. Falling is far different from the fate Alessandra suffered.

"Scott, why don't you start?" Dex suggests with his hand out at the scrawny man in front of him.

Scott shoves his fists inside his pants pockets and turns them inside out. His movements are unnecessarily aggressive, but at least his fists aren't finding anyone's face. Next, he pops open the buttons on his suit coat and pulls it open, revealing another ill-fitted shirt and a tie that's too short. But the undressing reveals nothing else—definitely not a large, iron key. In fact, he carries nothing sharp, not even a house key.

Slowly, we all start turning our pockets out, showing packets of gum, cell phones, and the gardening shears. Zyra explains she grabbed them when she was afraid Kaley was the killer. The group mumbles in understanding and we continue our scavenger hunt through pockets.

The poodle growls, but we ignore him. Maybe the lack of attention pisses the pooch off, because his vicious rumbling quickly builds to a shrill bark. Oscar pats Gassy's head, but the pup shakes his hand away, ears flapping. Gassy bares his sharp, yellowish teeth again, and it seems he's looking at Scott in the center of the group.

"What is it Gassy?" Darla says as she struggles to pull her purse off of her shoulder. I suspect it aches since she's complained of arthritis across all of her joints. She gasps as she follows the poodle's line of sight. "Gassy's right!"

We all take a pause to hear her out. It's a nice reprieve from emptying our pockets and exposing our weird quirks like the fact that I always carry paint swatches in my pants. And Zyra keeps a calculator on hand for good luck, even though every phone has one built in.

Darla jabs her finger at Scott. "You don't have the key because you stabbed Alessandra with a knife, didn't you?"

Scott coughs, suddenly choking on his own spit.

I forgot about the knife.

"The knife *was* missing from the table," Zyra says, chiming in with her sleuth skills. "I was inside getting a new one when I heard the scream."

Darla proudly pats her poodle's curly fur. "Good work, Gassy."

The Adam's apple on Scott's throat bobs and he finally catches his breath. "This is outrageous."

"I saw you by the cake," Darla says. She sounds confident but I can't remember him ever going to the food table after he first arrived. It stuck out to me since he complained about the lack of vegan hors d'oeuvres. Darla's memory must be muddled.

I scrape my own memory. If he wasn't at the table, where did Scott go after the group split up? Frank went to the bathroom, and I went to the speaker, but I didn't see Scott.

"I don't even eat cake; I'm vegan," he says. Spittle flies in Darla's face. She remains unbothered and only blinks casually at the angry man in front of her. "I never went to the food table, because I know events like this don't serve anything I can eat."

"That's actually true," Zyra speaks up again. She aims her calculator at Scott like a teacher's pointing stick. "I was tending the food table the whole time. I never served him."

"When did the knife go missing?" I ask.

Zyra shrugs, looking apologetic. I squeeze her arm against my side to show her that she has nothing to be sorry for. In fact, this is pertinent and useful information. As always, Zyra comes through with her observational skills and sharp thinking. I have no doubt she'll be the forensic scientist she dreams of becoming.

"If the knife is the murder weapon," she says, "someone must have taken it when I was busy talking. But I know Scott didn't come to the table, so there's no way he took the knife."

All at once, dozens of eyes land on Darla—the only one who has yet to empty her purse and the one with the very specific accusation. She's a gossip who talks more than enough to distract Zyra while she slips the knife away. The woman who has mysteriously outlived four husbands is definitely suspicious.

Only one question remains: what motive would drive Darla to kill Thorn House Road's HOA president?

13
IN THE SHADOWS WITH THE KNITTING NEEDLES

A whimper comes from beside Darla, but it's not the poodle who's making sounds. Oscar stares at the neighborhood gossip with brows furrowed and puppy-dog eyes. I never expected to see the resident war hero—the grumpy guy who literally yelled at me to get off his lawn when I was a kid—on the brink of tears.

Our silent, but clear suspicion of Darla has triggered something in Oscar. Is he in love with her?

I glance at Caspian, but his ghostly shape is gone. A gasp bubbles in my throat until I spy him beyond the group. Maybe to someone who is already dead, worrying about a killer isn't a high priority.

He waves at me from the end of the passageway and then points to an opening. "There's a clearing!"

I nod my acknowledgement. It's time to get moving.

"Let's see it," I say. I un-link my arm from Zyra's and point to Darla's bag. "Dump your purse."

Darla huffs, shooting an angry look around the group. Nobody jumps to her defense, or disagrees with my demand. Slowly, Jeanie, Frank, Scott, and Kaley all shuffle sideways or forward, unconsciously forming a misshapen oval around Darla. Everybody wants to get a look at the murderer's weapon, but it's tricky in the narrow space between sharp branches.

After a few moments, Darla sighs and yanks the top of her purse open. The magnetic button unhooks and, in an act of defiance, she flips the entire thing upside down.

Mints, lipstick, and a wallet rain down, disappearing into the tall weeds. She rolls her eyes and shakes the purse until more contents spill out. A ball of yarn drops to the ground and rolls to Zyra's shoes while something shiny follows. Sharp knitting needles fall at my feet.

I yelp and jump back before the pointy end can give my sandaled toes a piercing. One of the knitting needles stabs the soft soil where it sticks straight out of the ground. We blink at it for a moment before I reach for it.

Bodies press closer, clamoring to see if the hobby tool contains blood. I pull it from the dirt and we hold a collective breath as if I'm removing the sword from the legendary stone.

Other than mud, and the shine of the moonlight against the metal, the knitting needle is clean. I breathe again, which is ironic, considering the weapon and the murderer are still unknown. I'm not ready to see the tool that killed an innocent woman at my garden party.

I offer Darla the knitting needle. She snatches it from me with a huff and shoves it into her bag. Zyra, Oscar, and I stoop to help her retrieve the rest of the items.

Scott and Kaley argue in hushed tones while Frank announces he's not going to walk in front. I look up after collecting Darla's tin of mints and coins from her wallet to see Jeanie turn and lead the way, though she doesn't get very far before Frank pulls her back. Dex stands with his arms folded as he scans each of us.

I know he's trying to determine the killer—the person who deserves to walk with their back to us. We're all trying to determine the killer. Though Darla doesn't have the key or the knife and her knitting needles are clean, she's still a suspect. She could have stashed it after the stabbing, which means we still need to consider Jeanie a suspect too. Between the giant war hero, the gossip gal who points a finger at everyone else, the pageant mom with a secret, and the guy who punched Dex, we've hardly narrowed the list.

When I straighten, I wipe my hands on my pants and squint. Too many heads block my view of the end of the passageway. I shimmy back with my butt against the hedges to see past Oscar and the rest of the group. Caspian has left us behind. I catch sight of his leg disappearing around the corner.

Really? And I thought you needed me to help you solve your murder.

Not even a second later, a blast of cold air rushes me. The leaves rustle slightly and Caspian's transparent head appears from the hedges, inches from my face.

I swallow a gasp.

His disembodied head shifts to look at me. "I found the Lucky Bell!"

"The Lucky Bell?" I echo. It takes me a moment to remember the giant bell at the center of the maze. Once, a long, long time ago, Caspian and I snuck out this far. It was prom night, after all, and making out just didn't cut it. Not when he looked so dashing in a suit and tie. I drop my voice as low as possible and cock my head at him. "How did we get out here back then, but I can't find my way through now?"

Caspian juts a finger out of the hedges. "There were signs. The maze used to have wooden signs that guided you."

The fuzzy memory fills in. My mind's eye paints the picture of the quaint signs that read *this way*, *wrong way*, or *dead end*.

"That's right!" I say a little too loudly. Zyra glances at me.

For a moment, half of Caspian's body steps out of the hedges and he waves for me to follow him. "Come on, I think more of my memory is coming back!" In his excitement, he forgets I can't walk through walls of branches. Caspian's voice fades and I'm eager to see what he's found.

"I'll walk in front," I say, offering to be the Guinea pig. Really, I just want to catch up with the ghost who knows the way out. With my attention on the group again, they afford me mild interest. Kaley, Dex, and Zyra are the only ones who don't look suspicious. "But I didn't kill anybody!"

Murmurs ripple through the group, but I don't hear Kaley's shrill voice among them. When did she get on my side? I shake the distractions away and squeeze through the crowd of potential killers. I reach out and pull Zyra through the crowded space, the same way I always do when we pick our way to the front row of a busy concert.

Reluctantly, the rest of the partygoers follow. We have nowhere else to go but through.

My feet move faster the closer we get to the end of the narrow passageway. The moon casts light on the ground from the opening. I'm eager to get there before somebody can kill me and force me to walk into the metaphorical light. Not that I think they'll strike right here, right now in front of everyone else, but the threat creeps around the edges of my mind, anyway.

I'm nearly running as we reach the end and turn the corner. It's a breath of fresh air to step from the narrow hall of hedges into a clearing. The weeds are tall, but the little meadow is spacious and open enough to receive the moonlight. Towering hedges no longer crowd us and loom over our heads.

The clearing matches the size of a modern backyard in a suburban neighborhood. All it's missing is the signature barbeque, green turf, and the obligatory doormat. Instead, a replica of the famous Liberty Bell sits in the middle of the miniature meadow. A few large rocks surround it like benches, providing places to sit and admire the odd decoration. On the left and right are identical walls of thick hedges, and at the opposite end of the narrow passageway are five branching paths with more overgrown bushes.

My mouth hangs open as I approach the giant bell. I let go of Zyra and run my palm over the cool gold-painted metal while she continues on toward the paths. Quickly, she assesses the first one on the left, the darkest path where the moonlight can't seem to reach. Even a surprise bell in the middle of a maze can't derail her focus. She's the investigator I can only pretend to be. After inspecting the shadowy path, she moves on, poking her head into the second hall of hedges and looking around.

On the other side of the bell, Caspian materializes. He goes to knock his fist against the metal but it makes no sound and his face falls.

I smirk and rap my knuckles against it for him. A familiar clang echoes through the bell and a memory resurfaces.

"The Lucky Bell," I mumble, remembering the nickname Caspian and I gave the replica years ago. When we hooked up for the first and only time, we rang the bell, announcing to nobody that we got lucky that night. We fell over in the then-trimmed grass, giggling and snorting like the obnoxious, reckless punks we were. He always made me smile back then, and it wasn't until his parents refused to accept my pregnancy and their subsequent rejection that left me burying those memories and my feelings for Caspian.

"I forgot about this thing," he says.

"Me too." I look up and meet his gaze.

His smile has reached his dark eyes and I'm taken back a decade and a half. For one sad, sweet moment, we're young and in love again, alone in the center of his parents' giant, mysterious maze.

"But I remember more," he says. "There's definitely a way out down one of these. My father used to come out here, but he'd never leave through the front."

"What did he do out here?" My eyes trail to the five paths.

Caspian sighs. "I have no idea. He was a secretive man. He only ever brought Alessandra's father out here."

Alessandra's father? While that seems significant, I can't put my finger on the reason I need to question it further. The mystery surrounding this maze and his death isn't as important as the time-sensitive mystery of who killed one of us. Still, I'm curious and wonder if knowing more about Caspian's father will help answer what happened all those years ago. I open my mouth to ask what he thinks of it but noises interrupt me.

The moment between us dissipates as a dozen footsteps catch up. Everyone has found their voices. As they emerge from the narrow passageway, the hedges no longer mute the sound of gossip, complaints, and Gassy's growling. The commotion overwhelms me and scatters the focused curiosity in my mind.

I turn to face them. Between the bobbing heads and squawking about the long walk, they remind me of a gaggle of geese once again. Since I abandoned them, Kaley has resumed her spot at the front as the head goose, the leader of the V formation. She doesn't let the embarrassment of her husband's outburst or her exposed secret bring her down, and she's smarter for it.

What would have happened if I stayed tough like Kaley and didn't run from Thorn House Road all those years ago? Would Caspian have built a relationship with Zyra? Would my daughter know her father? Is there any way to reverse the damage that my cowardly escape has done? Caspian is dead, but he's not gone. Can Zyra ever meet him? The better question is if she even wants to. My daughter wants one thing and one thing only—to get into a good college that will jumpstart her career as a forensic scientist.

"What are you staring at?" Kaley asks.

She stands in front of me with her hands on her hips, and eyes narrowed. The stance doesn't intimidate me. In fact, Kaley's tilted head and furrowed brows denote curiosity, not anger. I blink and clear the daydreams of being the tough goose who flies against the resistance of the wind.

"You," I say, confessing the truth.

The rest of the geese fan out around us like we're rocks in the center of a stream. Frank and Jeanie come to inspect the bell while Scott follows Oscar and Dex to scope out the five branching pathways. Darla refuses to take another step. Instead, she stops in her tracks only a few feet from the narrow passageway. When she folds her arms, the straps from her purse dig into the soft flesh of her forearm.

"Obviously." Kaley shakes her head.

"What do you remember about Darla from when we were young?" I ask. Someone needs to verify whether Darla is capable of killing Alessandra. We need to narrow the suspect pool, and it's time I step up and do a little work. Zyra needs a mom who can ensure her safety. I wasn't brave when I got pregnant, but I can be brave now.

Surprised by the question, Kaley only blinks at me. A slight shade of black mascara coats her eyelashes. It matches the faint, dark line of eyeliner that's shaped to make her blue eyes appear larger. Though her makeup has mostly melted from sweat, I see evidence of the professional style that fits her personality.

"I mean, she outlived a few husbands, right?" I continue. "Could she have killed them?"

Kaley brushes a wisp of hair from her eyes and glances behind her. I follow her line of sight to the elderly woman who's scanning each and every one of us like she's the queen and we're her subjects. Darla purses her lips as her gaze lingers in one spot. Before I can see who she's glaring at, she notices us watching her and turns her head.

We snap our attention back to one another and Kaley flicks her eyebrows. "It's not a bad question," she admits. "But I don't see Darla as capable of stabbing someone. Plus, she and Alessandra got along just fine from what I know. Alessandra had tea with her every Tuesday morning. In fact, they spent a lot of time together, to the point where Alessandra referred to Darla as her adopted grandma."

A conversation like this is new to me. I'm not used to Kaley's respect, or kindness, or whatever this is. Her agreeable behavior is always reserved for people like Alessandra who were acceptable to wealthy folk either by name association, politics, or the number in their bank account. I never knew which piece of the puzzle graced Alessandra with the approval of Caspian's parents.

I guess living through a murder investigation really puts us all on a level playing field.

I tilt my head and release a hum. "For someone so close to Alessandra, Darla doesn't seem that upset," I say as I focus my gaze back on the woman in front of me. Red lines streak through the whites of Kaley's puffy eyes and a shade of pink tints her nose. "Shouldn't she be reacting the same as you? She seems more angry than sad."

Kaley sniffs and nods. "While that's true, Darla has no motive."

Before I can agree—another thing I never expected to do with Kaley Orange—the group crowds us. Zyra returns to my side while our neighbors surround the bell.

"Your daughter's a sharp investigator," Dex says from the other side of the Lucky Bell. Somehow he always ends up standing beside Caspian's apparition. Though their personalities are similar, I see the differences now. One is alive and warm, focused in an impressive career and kind enough to offer us his protection. The other, dead but not gone, still haunted by the fact that he never stood up for me and his daughter.

Caspian's frown is exacerbated by the sadness and lost look in his dark eyes. His arms hang limp at his sides, and his pained expression twists into something akin to grief. He's watching our daughter as she beams at Dex's compliment.

What looked like grief, I now recognize as regret. Because of his decision, and mine, he never knew Zyra. And that is truly the most depressing thing I can think of, because she's the most amazing person I've ever known. I've no doubt Caspian realizes this now.

Beside him, Dex folds his arms across his chest and nods at Zyra. "Tell her what you found."

Based on the smile she's suppressing, Zyra is secretly enjoying the opportunity to solve a crime in real life. "There's a wooden stake," she says, pointing to swaying weeds in the clearing. "Three signs have broken off of it, so there's no way to know where the arrows pointed. One says *gate entrance,* another says *outlet below*, and the last one is pretty faded but I think it says *liberty*.

"Like the liberty bell?" Kaley asks.

"Exactly like the liberty bell," Caspian chimes in though she cannot hear him. Sadness washes away, replaced by an epiphany. His faint ghostly lips almost curve into a smile. "My father used to say wealth is liberty."

I tilt my head ever so slightly and he looks up.

"Like financial freedom, I guess," he says. "Maybe that's why he liked this stupid replica. It was a symbol of his success motto."

While most of the group has turned to eye, the pathways and muse over which one has the outlet, I'm entranced by the ghost's realization, and Scott is busy looking at Frank. He nudges his bony elbow into his friend's ribcage and then nods at the bell. Frank seems to agree with whatever Scott suggested as he hands him the empty glass.

"Hold my beer," he says. With an amused smirk, Frank stoops to pull the clapper and ring the bell.

The loud chime echoes through the clearing, announcing the existence of the Lucky Bell for miles around.

"Frank!" Jeanie scolds with her hands over her ears.

Her husband shrugs and knocks his empty beer glass

against the top of the bell. "What? Maybe somebody will hear it and come let us out."

The swoop of Dex's hair flattens as he pushes the locks away from his face. In a voice as serious as Fox Mulder during an FBI investigation, he speaks up.

"Not likely," he says. "The plants are thick enough to block a lot of the sound, and Thorn House is too far from town. All our homes on this street are empty. There's nobody to hear it."

At that, I shiver. *Nobody to hear us.* And still so many suspects. I swallow a lump in my throat and link my arm through Zyra's again. I resolve to solve the murder, get us out alive, and get her the college essay topic of a lifetime. Caspian claims there's a way out down one of the pathways and I'm determined to get Zyra out through it.

Time to be brave, Olive.

"We need to split up," I say. It's a crazy plan, but it just might work. Caspian can lead us to the exit. We'll escape, and while Zyra is safe from confusing mazes and callous murderers, I'll get help for Dex, and Frank, and the other innocents, like Kaley.

"Excellent idea," Scott says, folding his wiry arms. His ill-fitted suit is tattered and torn from the hike through spiky branches. The sleeves still hang too long, almost covering his hands like he's a child wearing his big brother's hand-me-downs. "Let's get moving. Nobody will hear this old piece of trash." He kicks at the base of the bell, sending the sound echoing through the empty space inside.

"Our daughter is home." Jeanie says. "She might be able to hear it." Then with a wry smile, she glances around the circle. "She's studying for next year's beauty pageant interview."

"Nobody cares, Jeanie," Darla says, finally joining us

around the bell. But she doesn't become part of the clique. Instead, she turns her back to us—a bold move, really—and slumps onto a large rock before she yanks the clogs off of her feet and rubs her heel. Dry skin flakes off of her foot and floats down into the weeds like little flecks of snow. "Just like nobody cared that you cheated to make your daughter win last year's beauty pageant."

Jeanie's mouth falls open and I expect her to rip the glass from her husband's hands and dump the remaining drops of beer over Darla's crown of white hair. Apparently, Alessandra was right when she claimed Jeanie's secret isn't interesting enough to gossip about. Even Darla doesn't care for it.

In fact, she doesn't seem to care for anything except her feet and her dog. Where is her concern that a murderer is running loose?

For the first time in the history of ever, Kaley and I exchange a knowing glance. *Are you thinking what I'm thinking?* Based on how relaxed Darla is in the face of danger, she must know something we don't. Also, if Alessandra was like a granddaughter to her, why isn't she grieving? Was their friendship a facade like Kaley and Scott's marriage, or Dex's undercover alias? I'm tired of wasting time and wondering. These are questions I can't get answers to, so I focus on the plan of escape.

"As Dex said, it's just not likely anyone will hear the bell," I say. "Everybody pick a partner. Zyra and I will go together, of course. Check the pathways and then meet back here in a half hour to report what we find. There's a way out down one of these, and we'll find it faster apart."

It's bold, but heads nod, agreeing with the plan. Jeanie and Frank stand as if attached at the hip so I instruct them to the path on the far right. She agrees, likely eager to get away from the embarrassment caused by Darla's response. Frank sticks by his wife's side as they hurry to investigate what pathway number five has to offer.

"Are you okay flying solo?" I ask Dex. I don't want him to get hurt but I trust that he can hold his own as an officer of the law.

He shifts his jaw back and forth, considering this. "You two will be cautious?" His eyes flick from Zyra then back to me.

A warmth spreads through me at the concern in his voice. Dex is a good guy. I'm grateful he's stumbled into this mess even if it is my fault. I hope he can get his career back on track after the mistake that led him to Thorn House Road. Even though I wish him the success, it sucks that he'll be leaving when this is all said and done. I suppose it's for the best, Zyra already warned me not to break another guy's heart. Of course, Dex doesn't seem like the other dudes who get attached too quickly and then creep me out.

Speaking of unlikely couples, I spin around to face Darla. She sits still perched on the rock with Oscar standing like a bodyguard beside her.

"I assume you want to stick with Oscar since he's got Gassy?" I say.

Darla huffs. "I'm not going anywhere with anyone."

"You're saying you want to sit here alone while there's a murderer on the loose?"

She waves away my question. "Well, they're not going to kill *me*."

I resist the urge to look at Kaley. We have to be thinking the same thing now. The only way Darla can be so confident that she's safe is if she's the killer, right? In that case, I don't want to challenge her. If she stabbed Alessandra, what would she do to the person confronting her in front of the entire neighborhood?

I swallow my fear and dig up reminders of why I need to be brave. *Reason number one: Zyra. Reason number two: Zyra. Reason number three—*

Before I can repeat my daughter's name a third time and conjure a bit of courage, Kaley speaks up.

"Why aren't you sad for Alessandra?" Emotion cracks her voice, and her blonde bun that has unraveled into a messy ponytail whips to the side as she looks away. After a hard swallow, she focuses on the suspect.

Darla drops her bare foot. Her heel hits the ground with a thud and Gassy whimpers, sensing his owner's distress. The poodle scrambles and scratches Oscar's arm until he puts the pup down in the weeds. To my surprise, Gassy doesn't run to Darla. Instead, he picks his way through the tall grass finding a spot to crouch and take a quick bathroom break.

"I'm devastated," Darla says in a flat voice. "But when you've lived as long as I have, a dead body isn't so scary anymore. I've seen it three times now!" Darla holds up three fingers to emphasize her point. "All three of my husbands died before me, and even though it's been years, I still remember how death looks. It's just part of life."

Something doesn't add up, but I can't pinpoint what it is. Darla's statement sounds off and if I was a better investigator, I might identify the clue in her words. Instead, it takes me a whole minute to realize she forgot about tonight's dead body.

"Don't you mean you've seen death four times?" I say. "Because of Alessandra?"

"Right, yes," she says, quickly agreeing with my math.

Her white curls float forward and backward with her eager nod, like snow-colored cotton candy.

Oscar bends over and scoops the poodle into his arms. The entire time, he keeps his sharp gaze on Darla. "Five times," he says. "You had four husbands, Darla."

A little laugh escapes her. "I never considered you a husband," she says. "We merely dated."

Oscar gawps. Either the pup seeks to comfort him, or his cheek is tasty. Gassy cranes his neck to lick Oscar's face until his chin and cheek shines with poodle slobber. Absentmindedly, he pats Gassy's head.

"Dated?" he says. "Does that mean we're over?" Tears shine in the big war hero's eyes.

Tonight, everybody's true colors are coming out. Oscar is a sensitive softie, Dex isn't the farmer his clothes suggest, Scott's stronger than his scrawny body looks, and Kaley and I might even get along.

Either Oscar or the poodle whimpers; I can't tell where the sound comes from. The big guy looks like he needs a hug, but I don't make a move to comfort him just yet. He's glaring at Darla through a blur of tears.

"Now isn't the time, Oscar," she snaps. Darla is a conundrum, both on edge and too casual at the same time.

"I guess you'll forget me as easily as you forgot your last husband, huh?" He says as he clears his voice and shifts to pull a handkerchief from his pocket. With the poodle balanced in the crook of his large arm, his free hand to grips the lace handkerchief. The fabric is crumpled in his fist, but he uses the edge to dab at his eyes. "I should have known you're heartless. Who dates someone else when their husband isn't even cold yet? This is why I'm always a wedding officiant and never the groom."

I want to gasp at the scandal of it all, but I swallow the

inappropriate reaction. This isn't reality TV, and I'm not here to get distracted by drama.

Carefully, I piece the puzzle together. Darla dated Oscar after her husband's death. Or maybe *before* he passed away. If such an impropriety leaked in a town this judgmental, she'd surely lose her good graces with the elite crowd. Nobody with a lot of money wants to deal with someone scandalous. Rumors and lawsuits and drama cost something a lot more than wealth can buy—reputation. And here on Thorn House Road, reputation is everything. I know that as well as anyone else. After one prom night pregnancy, I bear the scarlet letter for the rest of my life.

Darla opens her mouth, but Oscar shakes his fistful of lace at her.

Before either of them can speak, I dive into the conversation head first. "Is that why you killed Alessandra?" I ask. I'm ready to uncover everyone else's secrets. Though I don't wish the shame I suffered on my worst enemy, exposing truth in a murder investigation saves lives. "Did she find out about your affair with Oscar and threaten to tell everyone?"

Darla freezes. Her wide eyes scan those of us still standing around the bell. Judging by the impatient focus on everyone's faces, it's obvious to more than just Kaley and me now—Darla Prune has something to hide.

"It wasn't an affair!" She finally squeaks out a response. The quiver in her voice further convinces me of her guilt.

Oscar shakes his head. "That's not true and I'm ashamed to admit it. You know we got together before he passed. You told me he was in a care home." His voice cracks and emotion chokes him.

I jump in. "This isn't adding up," I say, as if I don't suck at mathematics. But even I can solve simple equations:

defensiveness plus shock equals guilt. "What are you hiding, Darla?"

Finally, her face sags. The stretch of shock across her skin returns to her normal, tired expression with a hint of mischief.

A mixture of emotions swirls in my gut. I've confronted the guilty and I'm alive to tell the tale. But we're still trapped in here with the killer—my bravery hasn't saved my daughter yet.

"Fine," Darla says with a defeated shrug. "I've been lying this whole time."

14
A CONFESSION IN THE CLEARING

Getting a confession is easier than I thought. It's as if Darla enjoys spilling her tea. Sure, she delights in rumors, but I didn't expect she'd dump her own gossip so readily.

The exhaustion in her eyes vanishes and a smile tugs at her mouth where her red lipstick has long faded. Once she pulls her bare foot into her lap again, I wonder if she's done a few of Scott's cross-yoga videos. For her age, that level of flexibility is impressive.

"It was easy, really," she says as she rubs her thumb against her foot's arch. "I've been married so many times, I know exactly what a marriage license looks like and the process of getting one. With a little help on the technology side, I forged the license that connected me to a man who died upstate."

Gasps rippled through us, a wave of shock and admiration at Darla's impressive scam. But as interesting as it is, what does it have to do with Alessandra's death?

Oscar clears his throat and snuggles the poodle closer

to his chest. Ignoring Scott, he says to Darla "So you were never married a fourth time?" When Darla shakes her head, relief melts Oscar's pinched face. Gassy twists to lick the stubble on his chin again. It sounds like sandpaper rubbing splintered wood. "So it wasn't an affair..." His voice trails as his gaze sinks to her abandoned clogs in the weeds.

"What was the point?" I ask, eager to get the conversation moving. Now I understand why Darla confessed so easily—her crime is a scam, not a murder. The idea to split up and find the outlet is still our best plan of action and it's about time to get hustling.

After an exaggerated sigh, Darla looks up at me. Her eyes quickly flick to the poodle. "My precious baby takes a very expensive medication. I couldn't afford it. When I heard an old friend of mine was on hospice, I started rumors of us dating and a rushed wedding." A brief smile flashes on her face and then shifts to pinched lips. "Mr. Wodsworth really is a kind man. I would date him if he didn't smell like old socks."

Wodsworth? The name sounded so familiar. Did it belong to a man who once lived on Thorn House Road? No, Darla claimed he was from upstate. Or... *is* from upstate.

"Wait." I hold up my finger. "I thought your fake fourth husband died? You're talking like he's alive."

Darla nods. "I thought he died too. But apparently, the doctors misjudged his need for hospice and he's more stubborn than death. The marriage license still worked. Wodsworth couldn't remember if he married me or not, so I got access to all of his accounts and Gassy's condition was taken care of."

She shares information of this scam so freely that I wonder if she's not proud of herself. As I suspected, Darla has little shame. I suppose the poodle comes first and foremost in her life. To her, maybe any amount of trickery and lies are worth saving the pup's life.

"Wait." Kaley shoves past me. Though she's pushy and her brows are furrowed in the look of Oscar the Grouch, it's not directed at me. She glares at Darla. "Did you say Wodsworth?"

Darla's eyes almost pop out of her head. "No—"

"Yes, you did!" Kaley insists.

Zyra claps her hand over her mouth. I cock my head at her and mouth a question. *What am I missing?*

"Wodsworth," Zyra whispers. When I don't understand, she holds up her left hand and wiggles her ring fingers before miming the act of being stabbed.

Before I can stop myself, the words spill from my mouth. "Alessandra was going to marry Darla's fake husband?" My voice pitches higher with each word. Disbelief squeezes my throat. "On the same property that she was supposed to marry Caspian? What in the reality-TV-melodrama is this?"

Nobody answers me. Nobody even cares about my silly little outburst. Who's a decades-dead man to a group facing a present-day murder?

In a blur of shrieks, limbs, and choking cries, Kaley lunges for Darla's throat. But her thin fingers don't wrap around the elderly woman's neck; instead, she grips Darla's shoulders and shakes her.

Tears spill down Kaley's cheeks. "You killed her! You killed Alessandra for stealing your fake husband!"

While I'm frozen in place, Dex and Oscar dive forward to peel Kaley off of her. Since I'm the closest to Kaley and Darla, Oscar dumps the poodle into my arms. The pup's sharp claws scratch my wrist as he scrambles and wriggles, trying to jump back into Oscar's hold. My heart leaps to my throat in the chaos and the sight of a little blood beading on my wrist. The darn dog's panic left me bleeding and while I don't mind holding the adorable pooch, the sight of the red liquid makes me woozy.

I blink and try to make sense of the chaos.

Dex pulls Kaley back and pins her arms to her sides. Defeated, her shoulders drop and arms go limp while her chest rises with heaving breaths. Not even Jeanie or Kaley's own husband comes to her rescue, and it reminds me of the fake friends I made at the home improvement network—the type of people who follow you or stick by your side until the road gets bumpy and they ditch you on the side of it.

Oscar kneels in front of Darla and takes her hands into his. In another time and at another place, I'd believe I was witnessing a marriage proposal. But the fear creating more wrinkles on Oscar's leathery face isn't the expression of a future fiancé.

"What did you do, Darla?" he asks.

With bugged eyes, Darla averts his gaze and scans the group. She seems to be looking for something. At each face, she pauses for a moment and squints as if assessing our reactions. Finally, she faces the man in front of her and plucks her hands from his grip.

The breeze rustles through the clearing, sending the tallest of weeds swaying. They bow in the direction of Darla. She is the killer queen all along, not Kaley.

"I'm not saying another word." To seal the deal, she curls her lips under and folds her hands in her lap.

"I'm going to bury you," Kaley growls.

My eyebrows shoot up faster than a house falls during demolition. *Did she really just say that?*

"Bad choice of words," Caspian says, looking as shocked as I feel. Of course, it's hard to tell how pale a ghost has become. He's nearly impossible to see now, and I realize he's fading the closer we get to finding our way out. Will he disappear completely when we leave?

Dex clears his throat. "Um, Kaley—"

"I mean legally!" she says. Despite Dex's hold on her, she manages to lift one arm and wag her finger. "The moment we get out of this hellhole of a maze, I'll see you in court, Darla Prune."

As frightening as Kaley's threat is, Darla stays true to her promise. Her lips are locked tighter than the maze's iron gate. No antique key can pry the rest of the rumor from Darla now—much less the truth.

In the momentary silence, all I hear is the gentle rustle of leaves and a dozen people catching their breaths. The even rhythm of normal breathing tells me they're as relieved as I am. We've caught the killer and found a sign announcing the maze's exit.

If only the sign was still intact and the arrow pointed to the correct pathway.

"I'll see you in court..." Caspian breathes his icy words on the back of my neck. Goosebumps prickle over my neck and arms. I nearly jump out of my skin as he materializes behind me. "That's what Alessandra's father said to my father. I'd totally forgotten about that. That's why she was marrying me."

Forgetting about the poodle, the killer, and even the exit, I straighten and spin around. Caspian's face is upturned where the glow of the moonlight shines right through his transparent skull. His brow pinches in a serious look I rarely witnessed on him when we were young. He was carefree then, before whatever pressure his parents put on him.

"It was an arrangement between our fathers," he says. "I remember now. Her father found out my family hid money from the IRS. We didn't pay taxes on it, which meant my parents would go to jail for tax fraud. I even agreed to the deal, to marry her if her father kept our secret...until I didn't."

Before Caspian can share more, Dex touches my elbow and the goosebumps melt away. His heavy boots crush the weeds at our feet.

"We should find that outlet," he says. The warmth of his hand on my arm is a welcome relief from Caspian's lifeless chill. He nods at the scratch on my wrist. "Are you okay?"

I smile and say yes because it's the truth. Thankfully, the scratch is shallow enough that it only brought a speck or two of blood to the surface.

"Okay, let's hurry," Scott says, spinning around. "We're not getting any younger. I'll take the first pathway."

"We're going in pairs," Kaley says.

Her husband stops his forward march. "I-I figured you wouldn't want to team up with me."

Kaley shrugs. "I don't." Without hesitation, she chooses the spooky shadows over her annoying husband, and once again, I'm envious of her courage to face the darkness alone. Kaley doesn't think twice about confronting the woman who killed her friend or walking into the maze alone. Just to spite him, I suspect, Kaley selects the first pathway before Scott can get there.

Instead, Scott heads to the pathway that parallels the one she chose with a quick glance back. In a jerky movement, he waves for us to follow and then points to the remaining pathways before disappearing into the darkness.

"Take the third one," Caspian tells me. "That's the hatch."

Hatch? An underground escape matches the sign, *outlet below.* Caspian is getting Zyra and I to the escape.

"We'll take door number three," I say, pointing to the pathway in the middle. "Me and Zyra."

I reach for my daughter who quickly obliges and links her arm through mine. My heart swells. With her by my side, I feel a slice of the bravery I need to follow the ghost and get us out of here. But is it enough? Or am I just running away again? Zyra deserves to know her father.

I swallow and squint at Caspian's faint form.

He seems to understand my concern. "The closer we get to the exit, the more I remember...." Slowly, he raises his hands and then turns his palms out to show me how much they've faded. "And the less I exist. This is my escape too, I guess."

I blink away tears that threaten to pool in my eyes and give him a slight nod of recognition. With that, he moves toward the pathway, his form flickering along the way. It looks like he teleports through the weeds, disappearing and reappearing near the hedges. He turns and beckons for us to follow.

He's ready, so I don't waste another second. With my daughter at my side, I pull her along and hurry for the end of the maze.

"I'll stay behind and keep my eye on Darla," Oscar announces to those of us within earshot.

Now we have someone investigating each row and the bodyguard to watch Darla. For the first time a few hours, I'm feeling good about this neighborhood.

A white shirt catches the corner of my eye. Dex heads for his pathway, taking as long of strides as his tight jeans will allow. He stops before entering pathway number four and raises his voice with his hands cupped around his mouth. "If you find the outlet, come back and ring the bell. We'll all get out together."

Dem, he really is *a good guy.* Dex is looking out for everyone, though none of us are really his neighbors and he has another investigation to get to. He's more patient and selfless than I am. When we find the exit, I don't know if I can turn around and come back for everyone else. I'm sick of the sight of leaves and hedges and knowing that I'm trapped in a maze with a murderer.

We hike deeper into the corridor that's twice as narrow as the passageways that brought us here. Branches block the path but we kick through, ducking and weaving into small openings. Caspian moves fast, floating through any barriers.

In a matter of minutes, we come to a dead end. A tall, dark wall of leaves and spiky branches looms over us. I bite down on my phone, angling it so that the end with the flashlight is outside of my mouth and illuminating the ground beneath us. Carefully, we push branches out of the way in search of a hole or any kind of opening.

A mess of leaves, wildflowers, broken branches, and skittering bugs is all I see. A gasp dies in my throat at the sight of a black spider. I jump out of her way to be sure the tiny foot doesn't touch my toe. The spider disappears into the darkness of the hedges, and I almost wish I could follow her. These hedges are all that's stopping up from getting to safety.

After a desperate search, we both straighten and sigh. I wipe curls away from my face and give Zyra an apologetic look. If she could see Caspian, she'd know he's making the same face.

My heart drops to my stomach. There's no hatch, no outlet, no exit.

"I could have sworn this is the way," Caspian says. His voice is quiet, distant, though he stands right next to me.

Zyra steps back several feet from the dead end. She bends her knees, straightens, and then repeats the movement with a little hop. "Do you feel that?"

Before I can respond, she drops to all fours and clears branches and weeds away. Based on the sound of hinges straining under her weight, she's located the hatch. My heart pounds because I'm both excited to escape and proud of Zyra. Despite all of my mistakes and her father's poor choice, she's determined, smart, and tough. Maybe she doesn't need me to be brave. Maybe I just need to get out of her way and let her be the brave one while I support her every step.

"The CIA agent is right," Caspian says. "Our daughter is the sharpest tool in the shed."

I shake my head at him and let the smirk sneak onto my face. That's not exactly how Dex worded it, but I like Caspian's spin on the phrase.

"And it's all your doing." He smiles but I can barely see it. I'm grateful he's fading, not because I want him to leave, but because I can't accept the compliment. My gaze trails to her. Our daughter's intelligence and admirable traits have nothing to do with me. "You've got that look on your face like you don't believe me."

I keep my eyes on her. With a slight nod I signal that he's right, I don't believe it.

Zyra's not privy to her parent's private conversation. While we share a moment, she's yanking the hatch open.

The ugly plank looks familiar...I've seen the red wood stain before and I hated it then too. The plank falls open into the weeds and reveals a ladder leading into a dark tunnel.

"Should we get out and call the police?" Zyra asks, looking up at me through overgrown bangs.

I open my mouth to respond and a scream echoes through the night air.

15
SAVED BY THE BELL

For a full minute, I'm not sure if the panicked cry is coming from me. Finally, my brain registers that I'm silent and the scream echoes from the clearing. It's cut off quickly and, I fear, violently. One moment the woman's voice is shrill and desperate, and then the next, everything has fallen quiet.

Did Darla take a knitting needle to Oscar's throat? Has she slipped past him and followed Kaley to take her out with a whack of her heavy purse? Maybe Gassy is a trained attack dog, and she sent him to maul Scott or Jeanie. My mind reels with possibilities, real or otherwise. Thoughts flash so quickly they meld into one another before I can say a single word or move a single toe.

Zyra holds her palms over her mouth. She's straightened now, on her knees in front of the tunnel. Do we escape or go back for the second victim?

My heart skips a beat.

"Dex..." I say. As an officer of the law, he's the biggest liability to the killer. If Darla is as cunning as she's revealed so far, she may have slipped the gun from him. While it's not likely, the probability isn't zero, and I can't, in good conscience, abandon a possible victim.

Any goosebumps lingering from Caspian's chill melt away, and adrenaline leaves me hot and itching to take action.

"We can't leave him," Zyra agrees. The guy can hold his own, but we have the way out. While it's labeled an outlet, we have no idea where it leads or how long it will take. By the time we leave to get help and return, Darla could have killed them all.

"We can't leave any of them," I breathe.

The bell chimes, a low reverberating ring that's powerful enough to outshine the scream. It triggers me to run and my muscles obey. Zyra is on my heels, quickly passing me. She emerges from pathway number three first.

Fire burns in my lungs and my pathetic legs nearly give out when I reach the clearing. By the time I make it, my vision is blurred from breathing too hard. I double over, palms on my knees, and gulp as much air as possible.

Seconds later, Jeanie and Frank fly out of their chosen pathway, and I realize they're the last to arrive. Dex slowly approaches the center of the clearing with one hand at the gun on his hip. Scott and Kaley already stand over the body by the bell.

I blink away the blur in my eyes and make out the shape of someone crouching in the shadow of the Lucky Bell. Broad shoulders slump, and when he straightens, the moonlight shines off of Oscar's bald head.

"One... two..." I count the heads in a breathless whisper. Everyone is accounted for except the suspect. Where is Darla and who screamed?

Finally, my choking clears and I can get a chest full of

oxygen. I follow in Dex's wake with Zyra at my side. As my eyes adjust to the moonlight, I see her.

Darla lays sprawled on her stomach on the other side of the rock. It appears she fell, twisting on her way down. Unlike Alessandra, she's face down in the weeds, with limbs pulled close to her body as though she tried to break her fall.

Someone pushed her.

Thankfully, no blood trickles from the side of her head. She doesn't match Caspian—the other pushed victim.

"This means..." Zyra says under her breath.

"We didn't find the killer." I don't whisper. I want the whole group to hear. I want the killer to know we're not stunned. Despite the shock of it all, our brains have caught up with the situation.

An owl hoots from a nearby branch, adding to our spooky realization. When it takes flight, the flap of its wings fade into the night. If only we could fly out of here, we'd be safe.

"We were wrong," Jeanie wails. "And we're still trapped!"

"Nobody found the tunnel yet?" Scott asks.

Zyra nods. "Actually, we did; it's at the end of the center pathway."

"Oh." Frank palms his chest and lets his head roll back. The light of the moon streams over his face. "Thank heavens."

As usual, I'm frozen in fear or shock or whatever is the opposite of bravery. My daughter has to speak up to announce the good news through the frightening events.

Dex drops to the body, still the only one courageous enough to touch the dead. Now that I know he's an undercover agent, it makes sense how easily the investigation comes to him and why he didn't like me referring to him as a detective. Unknowingly, I almost outed him in front of the entire neighborhood. The agent places two fingers on the soft spot between Darla's neck and chin. Nobody breathes until he delivers the diagnosis.

"She's alive," he says.

Suddenly, the poodle releases a long, mournful howl followed by desperate whimpers. Despite the heat of bodies pressed close, the eerie sound gives me shivers. All at once, we look up at the man holding Darla's dog.

Oscar's wrinkled face smooths as his brows raise and the lines on his forehead fold into one layered lump. With Gassy perched in one arm, he holds the other hand up in surrender.

"Did you push her?" I say, thinking of how he claimed Caspian was pushed. Did Oscar have a connection to Caspian and Alessandra that we didn't know? His attachment to Darla is evident to everyone, and he gladly claimed the opportunity to stay with her. Alone.

Oscar's Adam's apple bobs. "I didn't," he says. A lot of people are claiming they haven't done a lot of things tonight. Thorn House Road is full of secrets, liars, and scandals. "Gassy wandered away. He's very particular about where he does his business."

"That sounds like a load of crap," I say with a joyless laugh. Zyra swats me, but Dex glances at me with the trace of a smirk on his lips. Another inappropriate comment at an inopportune time has slipped from me—story of my life. At least I amuse Dex.

"It's true," Oscar insists. "I was waiting for Gassy to finish when I heard her scream. I turned and saw someone in the shadows by the rock."

"Please, just step back," Dex says, calmly instructing

Oscar to move away from Darla. Carefully, he takes Darla's shoulders and rolls her to her side. She's breathless, but her eyes blink open.

"Someone p–pushed..." she struggles to speak at the awkward angle with her throat crooked and one arm crossed over her chest. Dirt stains the front of her beige sweater, and weeds are tangled in her fluffy white hair. Her fear is evident as she gasps, breathing only in fits of air as her lips quiver and eyes dart back and forth. A bruise blooms on her temple, and I'm reminded of Caspian's bloody head. This attack is the same MO with the push, the head injury, and at Thorn House.

Who has a vendetta against both Caspian and Darla? And what about Alessandra? How are the victims connected?

Dex helps her while Oscar dabs at the beading sweat where his hairline once was.

"Blood," somebody says. The word itself sends me into an instant dizzy spell, and I don't register who spied the red staining Oscar's handkerchief.

"It *is* blood!" Jeanie squeals.

I blink and take slow breaths to try to straighten the swaying world around me. My reaction to blood is getting worse, and it makes sense with the growing deaths and injuries I've witnessed. The spinning sensation has me convinced my head will float right off of my shoulder like a pinwheel.

Once my eyes adjust, I watch as Oscar slowly brings down the handkerchief. His tanned skin ripples to a stark shade of white. In seconds he's gone from the burly bodyguard, confident in his story, to as pale as the ghost beside me.

"You pushed her." I breathe. "Just like you pushed Caspian."

He doesn't acknowledge me, still staring at the red stain on the lace.

"Well?" Kaley says, pushing for answers.

In a collective, impatient silence, we hinge on Oscar's next words. His jaw hangs open, ready to respond. I swear we tilt forward as a group, moving like a school of fish with perfect synchronicity. Will he confess? Did Alessandra know about his affair with Darla? Did he kill Caspian for... what? I can't connect a motive, but it doesn't matter.

Instead of a verbal admission of guilt, Oscar exposes himself through action. He holds the poodle tightly to his chest and runs. Weeds crunch under his heavy weight as he leaves a path of broken plants in his wake. The poodle bounces up and down in his arms, and we all watch as he passes us. None of us are strong enough to stop the man who looks like a linebacker barreling down the field with a poodle-shaped football.

Jeanie squeals and jumps out of his way as he bolts for the pathway in the middle—the one with the exit.

"He's getting away," Kaley shouts.

Dex scrambles to go after him, but not without taking care to help Darla to her feet first. Our reactions are slow. Shock after twist after being locked together inside an endless maze has scrambled our brains and left our legs as tired as our emotions. I can't speak for everyone else, but I suspect this since we still move as a group, slower than we should.

The killer is escaping, and we're barely focused enough to stop him.

"Gassy!" Darla shrieks from behind us.

The gaggle of geese waddle after Dex, who enters the

pathway first. We squeeze in, following at his heels. The CIA agent has whipped out his gun now. He grips it in both hands and approaches the looming figure with his back to us.

"Stop!" Dex shouts.

Oscar doesn't listen, he nearly trips into the hatch. In the dim moonlight, I catch sight of his stumble before he rights himself and then crouches, ready to climb the ladder down into the darkness.

"Not another move," Dex says. "I don't want to shoot you."

At that, the murderer freezes. Bodies crowd the pathway, clamoring for a glimpse of the hatch, the killer, and the blood-soaked handkerchief in his hand. I shine my phone's flashlight on Oscar and grimace. My stomach flip flops and my head spins at the sight of the red on the lace.

Oscar has turned and raised his hand. The poodle whimpers and then tries to calm his handler with a few nervous licks on his sandpaper chin.

I can't seem to pull my gaze away from the handkerchief. The longer I stare at it, the less dizzy I feel and I wonder if my fear of blood is cured. Maybe having been haunted by a bloody ghost and witnessing a murder has made me brave. Or maybe that pale shade of red isn't blood at all.

I lean forward and squint. I'm so focused on the lace fabric that I don't realize I'm tilting off balance. Not only am I terrible at running, I'm clumsy too, and I can't catch myself before I stumble into Dex. Thankfully, he's solid as a rock and doesn't budge from his stance.

"Sorry," I say as he glances at me.

Caspian shakes his head and palms his face from his place between Oscar and the rest of us.

"I didn't hurt anybody," Oscar says.

"Then why did you run?" Dex asks.

"Because..." his face twists in fear as he uncurls his fingers. Between his thumb and forefinger, he pinches the edge of the handkerchief to give us a full view of the stain. "Someone must have planted this evidence."

"Wait," I say. "Just wait a second."

"Mom?" Zyra says.

I gently place a hand on Dex's forearm where his muscle is flexed to hold the gun steadily out in front of him. I raise my palms to signal *don't shoot.*

Carefully, maybe bravely—or stupidly—I take two steps toward the giant man, the tiny poodle, and the final clue. I beckon with two fingers for him to hand it over. Confusion washes over his face but he obliges. Once it's in my hands, I squeeze my eyes shut for a moment. If it's blood, I'll faint, if it's not...

With my eyes still closed, I bring it to my nose, and the familiar notes of citrus and red wine clue in my sense of smell.

"Oh my gosh," Zyra says, realizing what I'm doing. "It's not blood."

My eyes shoot open and I wave the scrap of fabric at Jeanie. "It's sangria."

"Right," Zyra agrees excitedly. This is it; we're almost to the end of the mystery. We've discovered another piece of the puzzle. Oscar was telling the truth. "Oscar was standing next to Darla when Jeanie threw her drink into her face! And then he offered her something to wipe it off."

Oscar visibly relaxes, shoulders slumping and breath returning to his heaving chest. It's clear we've all forgotten this in the midst of the chaos.

"Running is an act of guilt," Dex says, not totally

convinced yet. His weapon stays steady, pointed squarely at Oscar's chest.

"If not Oscar, then who pushed Darla?" Zyra adds.

"I remember the push now," Caspian says. With wide, dark eyes, he stares at nothing as if seeing the fall all over again. Carefully, he lifts his hand and gingerly touches at the wound on the side of his head. I've avoided looking at it this whole time, always keeping my gaze on his gorgeous eyes. "That's how I fell. I was pushed out the third-story window."

My eyes narrow as I turn to look up at Oscar. "You were with all three victims. Caspian, Alessandra, and Darla." I count off each one on my fingers to emphasize my point. They're connected, but I can't figure out how.

He shakes his head. "I never saw Caspian that day because the wedding never happened. I was at the altar the whole time, but the couple never came."

Of course Caspian never made it to the altar. He was busy plummeting to his death out of Thorn House's window. Shivers trickle down my back and I regret wearing sandals to tonight's gathering. Though I never could have predicted that the event's of my party would devolve into murder and a midnight hike through the maze. How can one dress for what they'd never expect?

"Gassy!" A quivering voice shrieks. Darla shoves her way through the crowd of neighbors, using her elbows to squeeze through Frank and Jeanie and emerge from the bodies. Her hands fly to her mouth. "Don't shoot," she begs. "He's holding my baby."

The words spill out of her as she shuffles forward. With her hands in a prayer, she pleads for Dex to put down the gun.

"Oscar's innocent," she says. "It was me. It's all my fault."

Didn't we already go through this? We suspected Darla; she clammed up, and then she got ganked. Unless she knocked herself out, her confession doesn't add up. Of course, I suck at math and I'm no detective. Maybe Zyra and her handy dandy calculator will figure it out.

Finally, Dex lowers his arms. Carefully, he lifts his shirt and tucks the weapon into his pants, all while keeping his eyes on Oscar. I rub my palm over my face and try to make sense of the mess of clues. The information is unfinished, like a puzzle from a garage sale with missing pieces.

Darla fans her face with her hand. Sweat trickles down her temples, making her bruise shine with wetness. "I never wanted Alessandra to get hurt," she cries. "I just wanted her not to go through with the scam. Wodsworth was *my* fake husband!"

"What?" I say it at the same time as Zyra, Dex, and Kaley.

Darla plucks the front of her sweater between two fingers and pulls it away from her chest. After repeating the process a few more times to pump fresh air on her skin, she clears her throat and continues. "Two days ago, an anonymous number text messaged me. They said they heard me arguing with Alessandra because she was stealing my source of money and I need to pay for Gassy's prescription!" Her voice pitches higher into a squeak. "The person who texted me offered to take care of Alessandra. So..." She swallows and looks at the group of people—one of whom sent her a sneaky text and a dangerous offer. I can't imagine how she must feel, having aided and abetted in Alessandra's murder. "I made a deal. I agreed to create a distraction at the party. During that time, they'd end Alessandra's reign over the neighborhood. I thought that meant she'd be exposed—you know, maybe this mysterious person had proof of her scam and they could embarrass her without bringing me down too. I thought it was just gossip! Not death. I didn't say anything this whole time because I didn't want to go to jail." She shoots her gaze to the whimpering pup. "I can't have my baby in jail with me. I just thought if we were stuck in here, I'd have enough time to figure out who did it..."

"What was the distraction?" I ask.

She waves her hand as if it's all a silly memory now. "The text told me to knock serving cutlery off the food table."

"The cake knife!" Zyra exclaims.

"Darla." Oscar's voice cracks. "If you needed money, you could have just asked."

She shakes her head and slaps her palm to her chest. Strained, she doesn't say another word. Instead, she digs into her purse—the bag that always hangs from her elbow—and produces her phone. After a few moments, she holds the screen out to show us proof of the text messages. The mysterious number isn't one I recognize, and nobody else jumps to identify it.

It finally makes sense. Darla was right next to me as we stood over Alessandra's body. She took the key and told us to look for evidence so she could lock us in and give herself time to find the person who used her to help commit a murder.

Tense suspicion returns. Everyone takes a step away from one another, despite the narrow space. They seem to prefer a branch in their backs over proximity to a potential killer. Which one of these people sent Darla the message?

I look up from the carabiner on my belt loop to Darla. "Do you have the key?" I ask.

Without another word, she yanks her purse open and pulls a flap of fabric out of the way, revealing a secret pocket. She plucks something in her fingers and lifts it out of the darkness.

The glow of the moon catches the black iron as she holds the key up.

I step forward and take it from her, returning it to its rightful place on my belt loop. All the while, Caspian's chill makes me colder and colder. He appears beside me, with his gaze locked on the antique key.

Free of its weight, Darla dives for her baby. Oscar helps the poodle jump into his owner's arms. While the pup snuggles into Darla's sweater, Oscar pulls his girlfriend into a hug. They stand inches away from the hatch, and I find myself staring at the darkness of the tunnel.

"I can't believe Darla made a deal with a killer," Caspian says in a quiet voice. "But I can totally believe Alessandra went for the marriage scam. It's just like when she was going to marry me—for a deal and for money. That's why I called it off." Sadness drags his face down, at least what I can still see of it. The more he remembers, the more he fades. "We never loved each other and I just couldn't go through with it. She was so mad..."

A gasp bubbles in my throat. Realization strikes me like a blow to the face. My heart starts pounding and blood rushes to my head, causing a lightning bolt of pain through my temple.

Alessandra was mad at Caspian, and it was Scott who went to speak with her. He was there... at Caspian's killing. *Which means Scott is the only one left alive who knows what happened that day.* He's likely a witness—or an accomplice.

16
AT THE TUNNEL WITH THE TEXTER

I stare at the ground, picturing the pieces of the puzzle. Caspian confirmed he saw Scott before he died, which matches Scott's story about seeking out Alessandra before the wedding.

But Scott swears he didn't kill Caspian, which leaves only one other person to push the groom out the window.

"Alessandra," I whisper. She was angry at Caspian for calling off the wedding. Did Scott attack Alessandra all these years later after gathering the courage to bring down a killer? Did he fear Alessandra might hurt Darla over their argument? Finally, I've realized the connection between both victims...and it's Scott.

I knew I wasn't Alessandra's biggest fan from the moment I met her at the first HOA meeting, but I never expected to accuse her of murder. It's the only order of events that makes sense. She wanted to marry Caspian for his family's money, and the deal to keep quiet gave her the opportunity. It's the same plan of attack she used to fake marry the wealthy man Darla was already trying to scam.

When Caspian refused, she got mad and shoved him

out the window. Why didn't Scott call for help? Did Alessandra threaten him too, and that's when he ran? If so, was her threat enough of a scare for him to kill her all these years later?

My eyes trail from my feet to the hatch in the ground, the only escape, the exit that Caspian's father must have taken whenever he'd enter the maze to make shady deals or do mysterious business. I raise my head and look right at the scrawny, cross-yoga influencer and speak loud enough for everyone to hear.

"Scott confronted Alessandra," I say, working the investigation out loud. "Oscar says he never saw Scott at the wedding and Kaley thought he left, but he already told us he was there. So where were you?" I need to get more information from him to clear up the last bits of confusion.

With an awkward laugh, Scott shrugs and glances around. "What do you mean? I just left. I didn't want to go to the wedding if she was going to go through with it."

I resist the temptation to give away my last piece of leverage. With all the strength in the world, I keep my gaze away from the hatch and fix it on Scott instead. Finally, for real this time, I'm facing the killer and I'm not going to back down. He ruined everything.

"Left?" I ask. "Which way did you go?"

"What are you talking about? I walked out the front door!"

I nod as if I believe him. "But Oscar and Kaley never saw you and the wedding took place in the front yard—"

"Maybe it was the back door." He scoffs. "I don't remember. It was a decade ago!"

The back door. Now I'm sure of it. I can't resist, my gaze flicks to the plank on the other side of the hatch. The red wood stain is the same shade as the mismatched planks on the deck by Thorn House's back door.

"This tunnel leads back to the house," I say, the words slipping from me and I can't stop what comes out next either. "I know because this is the same wood as the weird spot on the deck by the back door. You used it to escape after you witnessed Caspian's murder, didn't you? Or did you help the bride push him?"

Once and for all, Scott is speechless. No defense, no scoffs, or shrugs to brush off the accusation. He already admitted in front of the entire neighborhood that he was with Alessandra right before the wedding when Caspian fell to his death. Not to mention his blatant confession about how much he hated Caspian and wanted him to suffer.

Zyra's hands shoot up as she gasps. "Oh my goodness, Scott asked about the tunnel! When Darla was attacked, he called it a tunnel before we'd said anything. Plus, I bet the cake knife is the murder weapon," she says, pointing to Darla. "She unknowingly got the knife to Scott, and that's why I never saw him at the food table."

It isn't solid evidence, but it's enough to trigger Scott. His mouth hangs open and I almost expect a confession to fall out.

"Our daughter is amazing," Caspian says. "And it's obvious now, she *did* learn it all from you. I only wish I had gotten to know her."

An icy surface brushes over my hands. His ghostly, fading fingers slip into mine and he tries to squeeze, but his hand passes through my flesh and bones.

I look up to see tears in his eyes, and a sudden well of emotion chokes me.

"Thank you," he says, "for everything. It was crazy

brave of you to solve a ghost's murder." With a smirk and a curt nod, I realize he's encouraging me to continue.

I pull away from the freezing feeling and wipe a tear away from my eyes before anyone can see.

Then, I turn back to Scott. "You knew about the tunnel because that's how you escaped the wedding after you saw Alessandra kill Caspian. Maybe you even encouraged her to push him. I mean, you hated the guy since Kaley had the hots for him. I'm guessing Alessandra either threatened you for witnessing her crime or you're just as guilty of killing him and she wanted to pin it all on you."

Murmurs and startled shrieks overlap one another. I've dropped a bomb on them, and I can't blame them for the second round of shock that ripples over their faces.

For a moment, I let them soak in the intense information and turn to the man whose murder we've finally solved.

Caspian, my ex-boyfriend, the ghost haunting me, and my daughter's father, is gone.

17
OUT OF THE BASEMENT AT DAWN

My heart drops. As with other times, I expect Caspian to appear suddenly. Maybe he'll poke his head through the hedges or blink into existence beside me. I'll feel that familiar chill that I've grown used to and I'll find a way for Zyra to see him.

But he doesn't appear.

"Caspian?" I choke from the squeeze in my throat, and the sound barely comes out. His disappearance confirms my theory. The decade-old murder has been solved. Alessandra killed her fiancé on their wedding day by pushing him out of a third-story window.

It's done.

Caspian's gone.

Time for me to move on.

To my surprise, the thought doesn't hurt. Moving on doesn't dredge up feelings of regret and sadness and open-ended questions. Caspian made a mistake. He was a coward and followed his father's demands instead of building a relationship with his own daughter. But I'm no better. I ran from Thorn House Road at the first sign of judgment and whisked Zyra away from any chance of knowing the other half of her family.

I don't hold this against Caspian anymore. I don't even hold it against myself anymore.

Because it's finally time to move on.

I still don't agree that I was brave, but it's okay. Despite my and Caspian's mistakes, Zyra turned out far better than I could have ever imagined.

"You forgot," Zyra says to me and I realize only seconds have passed since I announced my theory about the murder. "Scott also kept pushing for us to split up, probably to find the tunnel."

That's true. Why did Scott stick around and whack Darla when she didn't seem to know who sent the text messages?

Too curious for my own good, I ask, "if you knew where the tunnel was, why not just escape without us?"

Scott's nostrils flare like a bull ready to trample me and I worry curiosity will kill Olive the cat, if I'm not careful. A twitch flickers on his thin lips. They match the rest of his cross-yoga body where lean muscles make him look slightly emaciated. "Because I knew that stupid old witch had the key hidden somewhere. It was my ticket to freedom while you idiots bumbled around looking for a buried tunnel. But I didn't account for her personal bodyguard to be with her at all times." Scott sneers at Oscar who doesn't take the bait. The giant man has returned to his stoic status, folding his emotional, sensitive side under layers of leathery wrinkles and a flat expression. "Thankfully, that rat needed to take a dump." Spit flies from between Scott's slightly crooked teeth.

Gassy growls at the rude name-calling and releases a

hoarse bark. Moonlight shines against the poodle's sharp canines until Oscar gently calms him with soothing pets and Gassy stops growling. Maybe the war hero's sensitive side isn't so hidden.

"But you could have just escaped through the tunnel," I say, though I know it will probably piss him off. After all of this, I still don't have control over my mouth. There are some things I'll never learn.

Scott scoffs. "It's been ten years. Do you really think I remembered which path it was in? I have more important things to think about than this hideous old place and your baby daddy's drama."

Apparently, you don't. Scott made it his business to poke his nose into Caspian's non-love life and it got him involved in a murder, and then committing one several years later.

"I'm ready to get this show on the road," Dex says and waves the gun at Scott.

"Told you he has a gun," Kaley says, which prompts Dex to explain his status as a CIA agent. His skill with words keeps the details of his investigation vague while satisfying the neighbor's curiosity.

Thankfully, my embarrassing and illegal social media purchase isn't exposed.

Zyra moves toward me, ducking out of Dex's way as he instructs the murderer to turn around. Everyone accepts this and allows the agent to take over because it's a long time coming.

We knew someone killed Alessandra, and the truth has finally come out. To our good luck—and Dex's bad luck—he was led here through confusing clues and now we have an officer of the law to detain the dangerous yoga influencer. Maybe if Scott never mixed yoga with aerobic exercises, he'd have the zen to control his temper and Alessandra would still be alive. Maybe if he wasn't dishonest himself, he could have talked her out of the lie and convinced her to come clean.

There are too many *what if* questions and I file them away in the recesses of my brain. I'm tired of asking *what if* in my own life. What's done is done and we can only make the best with what we have.

"You can't take the law into your own hands," Dex says as he grips Scott's arm. "If Alessandra killed this other guy, there should have been a trial, not a stabbing."

We nod along, breathing with ease now that everything is exposed. While I don't wish for anyone to feel embarrassed, it's also nice to know the people of Thorn House Road have secrets. I'm not the only one haunted by mistakes of the past. I never should have taken Zyra away from her father to protect myself from judgments, but we're back now and I vow to make the best of it.

I scan my neighbors and their various reactions to the big reveal. Kaley has her arms crossed, and she shakes her head at her disappointing husband. Darla buries her face in Oscar's chest while she cries with the realization that Scott was the one who tricked her. Jeanie and Frank watch with mild amusement and relief.

"Wait!" Scott shouts. In a fiery explosion of a hot temper, he yanks free from Dex's hold and throws his hands out wide as if we're a group of velociraptors ready to pounce on him. "This isn't my fault."

"Mm-hmm," Dex says, but he continues to signal Scott to turn around with the barrel of his gun.

"I'm serious!" Scott touches his temples with unsteady fingers. "Alessandra killed Caspian," he says. "You all know that now, right?"

Again, we nod.

"I was merely a witness." He's breathless and speaks only between gasps and a quick lick of his lips. "I saw it. Right? I just saw it. I didn't push him."

"But you stabbed Alessandra," I say.

"With the cake knife," Zyra adds.

"In the rose bushes," Dex finishes. "So we're going to hold you until the police come to make a final arrest for murder."

"No, no, no." Scott shakes his head. "You're not listening. Alessandra was feeling guilty for killing Caspian. I guess this stupid fake wedding she was planning brought up all those feelings or something. She just wanted to pretend it never happened, so she came to me and asked me to lie and say I saw the whole accident so she could clear herself from it once and for all."

"So you killed her," I say.

"At our party," Zyra adds.

Dex opens his mouth to throw in his two cents but Scott doesn't allow for another round of that nonsense.

The killer throws up his hands and groans. "Yes, I killed her, because she was a killer! And Olive clearly wanted her dead anyway, which means it's basically her fault." He shouts the latter part of the sentence to emphasize his point. Maybe he thinks stabbing someone is a good deed since the twist reveals she wasn't an innocent woman.

My eyes bulge and I worry they'll pop right out of my skull and roll down the pathway into the tunnel. I blink, speechless at his accusation. The beat of my heart thuds erratically. If they knew me better, they would know I can't so much as think of blood without getting woozy—much less stab someone in the heart.

"N-no." I clear my throat. "I didn't want her dead. I only wanted her HOA president's stamp of approval!"

"Oh, come on." Scott rolls up his sleeves but I don't fear he'll punch me because Dex is right beside him. "She was going to marry the ex-boyfriend who dumped you *and* she snubbed your HOA request in front of everybody."

So I really *was* framed. Almost. Thank goodness for Darla locking us in here and Dex's attendance, or else Scott might have gotten away with it. Everybody was a little buzzed and Zyra was inside looking for a new knife. The muddled timeline of events and everyone's placements is hazy enough to have tripped up a jury.

"Pfft." Kaley makes a raspberry with her lips and rolls her eyes at her husband. "You killed her because you have a horrible temper and all you care about is your reputation as the enlightened influencer. Concealing a murder won't look so good to your YouTube followers." With a flick of her head and a wave of her hand, she gestures for Dex to detain her husband. "Make him walk in front. He's a liar. Did you all know he's not even vegan? He eats steak at least twice a week and made me swear never to tell anyone."

Dex nods and proceeds to grab Scott. The wiry guy wriggles and squirms, but he's no match for the CIA agent's strength.

I allow myself a moment to admire Dex's arm muscles as he pulls Scott's hands behind his back.

Finally, Darla's plan—the good one—is in motion. The killer walks up front with his back to us and the barrel of Dex's gun pointed at his spine. One by one, Oscar helps us down into the tunnel where we whip out our phone's flashlights.

Though we have the gate's key, we decide a straight tunnel is likely the faster route out of a winding maze. Scott mumbles and groans as Dex prods him along. The tunnel is spooky, but I swallow my fear and we make our way through the underground passage.

Time moves slowly in the darkness.

Zyra leans close to me and whispers. "Do you really think Scott believed he was doing the right thing? Like, seeking justice for my dad's death?"

I wrap my arm around her and gently my bump my head against hers. "I think we'll never know what really happened that day. Scott hated Caspian, and he was with Alessandra when she pushed him. Maybe he helped her. Maybe he even convinced her to do it. The whole thing is baffling, but he's smart enough to know that dredging it up again and lying about the events was going to get him in trouble."

"But not smart enough not to kill her over it," she adds.

"Exactly."

And not smart enough to let us believe Darla was the suspect. Of course, jumping into an attack fueled by a bad temper matched Scott's MO. The guy just couldn't keep his hands off of people. He was willing to do anything to protect his reputation and keep Alessandra quiet—even kill.

Though the dark underground trek is chilly, I no longer shiver. The ghost is released to rest, and the murder solved. The damp, old tunnel smells musty and more than a few spiders skitter away from the light of our phones. We walk on and on as a single-file train, waiting for this night to end.

Finally, the tunnel opens into a spacious room. Dex keeps his weapon trained on the killer while we fan out and look around the room. It appears we've arrived underneath the house, and this is a basement used for storage. White sheets cover stacks of bins full of tea lights, lanterns, and other, more lavish wedding decorations.

Kaley opens a box and pulls out a lace tablecloth. "It's such a shame this has all gone to waste. Their wedding was going to be so beautiful."

"But fake," Darla says. "Alessandra just wanted his money like she wanted Wodsworth's will."

Kaley hums in agreement.

"Maybe it doesn't have to go to waste?" I say as I step up beside the next person I believe will take over Thorn House Road's Homeowners' Association.

Kaley purses her lips and gives me the side-eye. Finally, she nods and her ponytail wiggles from the movement. "Maybe."

"I'm sorry about Scott," I say, unsure of how to broach the subject. Kaley's example of strength and leadership tonight has me wishing we were closer. I admire her and need more of that positive influence, though I never thought it'd come from Kaley Orange.

With a brush of wispy hair that hangs in her face, she straightens. Her posture isn't rigid or that of a snob, but the poise of an independent woman. "He was a good house husband," she says with a flick of her head. "I kept him around because he can grill a steak to perfection and he's the only one I trust to steam clean my Persian rugs. But it will be nice not to pretend anymore. I suppose I owe you an apology for going after Caspian when we were kids."

I wave the suggestion away. "We were young and dumb."

"Oh, I wasn't dumb," she says. "Caspian Blanc was a rare catch, wealthy and kind. That's why Alessandra and I became such good friends. Great minds think alike...or so I thought. It's such a disappointment to hear she stooped low enough to scam these men. Now *that* is dumb and wrong. What I did...." Her gaze glazes and she sighs. "What I did was just plain wrong and I'm sorry for it." Lace table runners fill the clear bin where her eyes are fixed. For a moment, she flicks her attention to me and then sniffs. "Anyway, it seems I need to select my friends more carefully."

Am I about to become friends with a lifelong Thorn House Road resident? It seems impossible but we've all changed a little tonight. At least, I suspect we have. Secrets were exposed, and the truth means we no longer have to keep up facades.

Oscar announces he's found the ladder that leads up and out of the basement. As I suspected, the mismatched planks on the deck are the opening that leads out of the underground space. He pushes the hatch open and we blink at the bright morning light that floods in.

Once we climb out of the basement, I find Zyra standing in the middle of the yard. The party is a mess of spoiled food and napkins blown around the grass from the wind. The speaker registers my phone's connection again and faintly plays a classy jazz tune from my party playlist.

I walk up to my daughter and link my arm through hers.

"Don't look down," she says as she goes to cover my eyes.

"What is it?" Panic rises in my chest.

"The murder weapon. I found the cake knife, and it's, well..."

I raise my hand to stop her from saying the word. Apparently, I'm not cured of my fear of blood. Even the thought of it makes my head spin.

"I can be brave," I say. Maybe it's a lie, but I want to try.

"You don't need to be brave," she says. "Not until our next event, anyway." A twinkle shines in her eye. "Real charcuterie boards, remember?"

"Real charcuterie boards," I say, pronouncing it correctly for the first time.

18

THE DECISION AT THE HOA MEETING

Two months after Scott's arrest, Thorn House Road's HOA meetings resume. We've gathered in the backyard again. Since the night of the garden party, I got the creepy fence removed, replanted the rose bushes, and demolished the deck. Even the maze is trimmed and looks like an asset to the lovely yard.

After stepping down from the CIA to become a local police officer, Dex took a brief vacation during the time in between. Together, we built and painted signs to scatter throughout the maze, and I didn't have to ask Zyra for help.

She stayed focused on her studies, preparing for college the best way she knew how. Though Dex's vacation inspired her to take breaks every now and then. When she didn't have her nose in a book, Zyra enjoyed planning event menus.

Tonight is warm, so I've placed tall stakes in the ground and lit them with a flame meant to drive away mosquitoes. The flickering glow gives the yard an ethereal ambiance only enhanced by the fairy lights that I've strung all throughout the maze.

We sit around the iron table where grapes, cheeses, and crackers fill charcuterie boards. I smile at Zyra, who has a textbook open in front of her on the table. With a pencil in one hand and a slice of cheese in the other, she fuels her studying.

"So." Kaley claps her hands and stands at the head of the table. "I've counted the votes."

Zyra looks up and reaches for my hand. Across the table, she squeezes my fingers and gives me all I need to be brave. Even if we end up having to demolish Thorn House, I'll be okay. Just like with the maze, we always find a way out of trouble. I won't give up until Zyra's college account is filled with funds for her Harvard tuition.

"It's unanimous," the new HOA president says. My heart skips a beat and my life's plans hinge on her next words. Will I become the official hostess of Thorn House Events Center, or will we have to move on from here and start from scratch? "Thorn House will stay standing."

Zyra shakes my hand and my head droops in relief. When she lets go, she turns a page in the textbook and resumes her study session.

A broad smile spreads over Kaley's face. "Maybe we'll even have a wedding here soon?" Thankfully, her gaze passes over me and Dex and lands on the couple at the other end of the table. Dex and I have only just started dating, which means neither of us is ready to discuss marriage.

I follow Kaley's line of sight to where Darla leans her head on Oscar's shoulder. With Kaley as her lawyer, she's likely to get off with community service, and while she serves her time cleaning up trash along the road, Oscar has promised to keep Gassy safe and give the poodle his daily dose of medication.

"Or you could hold a beauty pageant," Jeanie suggests.

"Nobody cares, Jeanie," Darla says. Despite everything that's happened, Darla remains her feisty, gossip-loving self.

I crane my neck to see Jeanie's beehive of red hair at the opposite side of the table. "I care," I say. "Just say when and I'll host."

At that, Jeanie blushes and settles happily into her chair while Frank nurses a glass of beer beside her. The foamy golden liquid sloshes around in the glass as he raises it to make an offbeat toast.

"To Thorn House parties," he says. "If this ol' wreck can get approved, my backyard Ferris wheel should be next."

Jeanie swats him, but he's unbothered and takes a gulp of beer. Despite the drama that HOA meetings often bring, we're enjoying ourselves. The wine is delicious, the charcuterie boards look divine, and Dex's warm hand finds mine.

Already, my promise to the former HOA president to create new memories—good memories—and replace Thorn House's poor reputation, is underway. I don't have to demolish the beautiful, old building, and Zyra gets to keep this piece of her father.

It doesn't fix the mistakes of the past, but we move on, and I vow to help my new friend and HOA president, Kaley, make our neighborhood a great place to live.

A cool breeze blows through the yard, and I know Caspian agrees. Thorn House is no longer the residence of snooty, judgmental people with secrets to hide, but an event center for celebrations.

I keep an open-gate policy. All are welcome to come party at Thorn House—even ghosts.

Now that Thorn House Events Center is officially approved, it's time to let the games begin. Unfortunately, bridezillas and a summer thunderstorm aren't the only things haunting the third wedding hosted by Thorn House. When the wedding party gets locked inside, it's up to Olive, Zyra, and Dex to uncover the truth before another body drops.

Please consider leaving a review at your favorite place to purchase books! Also, a share with your friends who love to laugh and solve mysteries would be greatly appreciated. My quest as an author is to make others feel seen through the adventure of fiction. Please reach out to me and let me know if my stories have touched you. You, dear reader, are who this book was written for.

ABOUT THE AUTHOR

Congenital Heart Defect survivor, Emily Fluke, finds joy and peace through the expression of writing. She is a firm believer that all stories need a little magic and a lot of excitement. Emily and her husband spend their free time wrangling two children and playing video games in their busy California lifestyle. Otherwise, you'll find Emily solving an escape room, running, or writing Magic the Gathering-based poetry.

To stay up to date on new releases and connect with me, visit my website at Emilyfluke.com or follow me on social media under Author Emily Fluke, or @emilyflukefairytales.

www.ingramcontent.com/pod-product-compliance
Lightning Source LLC
La Vergne TN
LVHW090518110826
845146LV00003B/909

* 9 7 9 8 9 8 5 5 4 7 3 8 2 *